Breakfast in the Ruins

*Also by Michael Moorcock and
available from New English Library:*

CITY OF THE BEAST

LORD OF THE SPIDERS

Breakfast in the Ruins

A Novel of Inhumanity
by Michael Moorcock

NEW ENGLISH LIBRARY
TIMES MIRROR

First published in Great Britain in 1972 by
New English Library Ltd

٭

© Michael Moorcock 1971

٭

FIRST NEL PAPERBACK EDITION MARCH 1973
New edition April 1975
This new edition September 1978

٭

NEL Books are published by New English Library Limited from Barnard's Inn,
Holborn, London EC1N 2JR. Made and printed in Great Britain by C. Nicholls &
Company Ltd.

4500 4152 2

For Angus Wilson with great respect

CONTENTS

Introduction

Michael Moorcock died of lung cancer, aged 31, in Birmingham last year. The whereabouts of Karl Glogauer are presently unknown.

JAMES COLVIN

Three Chimneys,
Raddon, Yorkshire.

1

In The Roof Garden: 1971: Scarlet Sin

Commonwealth immigrants to Britain were 22 per cent down in April. There were 1,991 compared with 2,560 in April last year.

THE GUARDIAN, *June 25, 1971.*

WHEN in doubt, Karl Glogauer would always return to Derry and Toms. He would walk down Kensington Church Street in the summer sunshine, ignoring the boutiques and coffee shops, until he reached the High Street. He would pass the first of the three great department stores which stood side by side to each other, stern and eternal and bountiful, blotting out the sky, and would go through the tall glass doors of the second store, Derry's. The strongest of the citadels.

Weaving his way between the bright counters, piled with hats and silks and paper flowers, he would reach the lifts with their late art nouveau brasswork and he would take one of them up to the third floor – a little journey through time, for here it was all art deco and Cunard style pastel plastics which he could admire for their own sake as he waited for the special lift which would come and bear him up into the paradise of the roof garden.

The gate would open to reveal something like a small

conservatory in which two pleasant middle-aged ladies stood to greet the new arrivals and sell them, if required, tea-towels, postcards and guide books. To one of these ladies Karl would hand his shilling and stroll through into the Spanish Garden where fountains splashed and well-tended exotic plants and flowers grew. Karl had a bench near the central fountain. If it was occupied when he arrived, he would stroll around for a while until it was free, then he would sit down, open his book and pretend to read. The wall behind him was lined with deep, airy cages. Sometimes these cages were completely deserted but at other times they would contain a few parrots, parrakeets, canaries, cockatoos, or a mynah bird. Occasionally pink flamingos were present, parading awkwardly about the garden, wading through the tiny artificial streams. All these birds were, on the whole, decently silent, almost gloomy, offering hardly any reaction to the middle-aged ladies who liked to approach them and coo at them in pathetic, sometimes desperate, tones.

If the sunshine were warm and the number of visitors small Karl would sit in his seat for the best part of a morning or an afternoon before taking his lunch or tea in the roof garden restaurant. All the waitresses knew him well enough to offer a tight smile of recognition while continuing to wonder what a slightly seedy looking young man in an old tweed jacket and rumpled flannels found to attract him in the roof garden. Karl recognised their puzzlement and took pleasure in it.

Karl knew why he liked to come here. In the whole of London this was the only place where he could find the peace he identified with the peace of his early childhood, the peace of ignorance (or "innocence" as he preferred to call it). He had been born at the outbreak of the war, but he thought of his childhood as having existed a few years earlier, in the mid-thirties. Only lately had he come to understand that this peace was not really peace, but rather a sense of cosiness, the unique creation of a dying middle-class. Vulgarity given a gloss of "good taste". Outside London there were a few other spots like it. He had found the right

12

atmosphere in the tea-gardens of Surrey and Sussex, the parks in the richer suburbs of Dorking, Hove and Haywards Heath, all created during the twenties and thirties when, to that same middle-class, comfiness had been a synonym for beauty. For all he knew too well that the urge which took him so frequently to the roof garden was both infantile and escapist, he tolerated it in himself. He would console himself sardonically that, of all his other infantile and escapist pursuits – his collection of children's books, his model soldiers – this was the cheapest. He no longer made any serious attempts to rid himself of these unmanly habits. He was their slave, just as much as he was the slave of his mother's childhood terrors; of the rich variety of horrors she had managed to introduce into his own childhood.

Thinking about his childhood as he sat in his usual place on a soft summer's day in June 1971, Karl wondered if his somewhat small creative gift was not, as most people would nowadays think, the result of his unstable upbringing at all. Perhaps, by virtue of his sensitivity, he had been unduly prone to his mother's influence. Such an influence could actually stunt talent, maybe. He did not like the drift of his thoughts. To follow their implications would be to offset the effects of the garden. He smiled to himself and leaned back, breathing in the heavy scent of snapdragons and tulips, believing, as he always did, that it was enough to admit a self-deception. It was what he called self-knowledge. He peered up at the blue, uncluttered afternoon sky. The hum of the traffic in the street far below could almost be the sound of summer insects in a country garden. A country garden, long ago . . .

He leaned back on the bench a fraction more. He did not want to think about his mother, his childhood as it actually was, the failure of his ambitions. He became a handsome young aristocrat. He was a Regency buck relaxing from the wild London round of politics, gambling, duelling and women. He had just come down to his Somerset estate and had been greeted by his delightful young wife. He had married a sweet girl from these parts, the daughter of an old-fashioned squire, and she was ecstatic that he had returned home, for she doted on him. It did not occur to her to criticise the way he chose to live. As far as she was concerned, she existed entirely for his pleasure. What was her name? Emma? Sophy? Or something a little more Greek, perhaps?

The reverie was just beginning to develop into a full-scale fantasy when it was interrupted.

"Good afternoon." The voice was deep, slightly hesitant, husky. It shocked him and he opened his eyes.

The face was quite close to his. Its owner was leaning down and its expression was amused. The face was as dark and shining as ancient mahogany; almost black.

"Do you mind if I join you on this bench?" The tall black man sat down firmly.

Frustrated by the interruption Karl pretended an interest in a paving stone at his feet. He hated people who tried to talk to him here, particularly when they broke into his daydreams.

"Not at all," he said. "I was just leaving.' It was his usual reply. He adjusted the frayed cuff of his jacket.

"I'm visiting London," said the black man. His own light suit was elegantly cut, a subtle silvery grey. Silk, Karl supposed. All the mans clothes and jewellery were evidently expensive. A rich American tourist, thought Karl (who had no ear for accents). "I hadn't expected to find a place like this in the middle of your city," the man continued. "I saw a sign and followed it. Do you like it here?"

Karl shrugged.

The man laughed, removing the cover from his Rolleiflex. "Can I take a picture of you here?"

And now Karl was flattered. Nobody had ever volunteered to take his picture before. His anger began to dissipate.

"It gives life to a photograph. It shows that I took it myself. Otherwise I might just as well buy the postcards, eh?"

Karl rose to go. But it seemed that the black man had misinterpreted the movement. "You are a Londoner, aren't you?" He smiled, his deep-set eyes looking searchingly into

Karl's face. Karl wondered for a moment if the question had some additional meaning he hadn't divined.

"Yes, I am." He frowned.

Only now did the elegant negro seem to realise Karl's displeasure. "I'm sorry if I'm imposing . . ." he said.

Again, Karl shrugged.

"It would not take a moment. I only asked if you were a Londoner because I don't wish to make the mistake of taking a picture of a typical Englishman and then you tell me you are French or something!" He laughed heartily. "You see?"

Karl didn't much care for the "typical", but he was disarmed by the man's charm. He smiled. The black man got up, put a hand on Karl's shoulder and guided him gently to the fountain. "If you could sit on the rim for a moment . . ." He backed away and peered into his viewfinder, standing with his legs spread wide and his heels on the very edge of the flower bed, taking, from slightly different angles, a whole series of photographs. Karl was embarrassed. He felt that the situation was odd, but he could not define why it should seem so. It was as if the ritual of photography was a hint at a much more profound ritual going on at the same time. He must leave. Even the click and the whirr of the camera seemed to have a significant meaning.

"That's fine." The photographer looked up. He narrowed his eyes against the sunlight. "Just one more. I'm over here from Nigeria for a few days. Unfortunately it's more of a business visit than a pleasure trip: trying to get your government to pay a better price for our copper. What do you do?"

Karl waved a hand. "Oh, nothing much. Look here, I must . . ."

"Come now! With a face as interesting as yours, you must do something equally interesting!"

"I'm a painter. An illustrator, really." Again Karl was flattered by the attention. He had an impulse to tell the man anything he wanted to know – to tell him far more, probably, than he was prepared to listen to. Karl felt he was making a fool of himself.

15

"An artist! Very good. What sort of things do you paint?"

"I make my living doing military uniforms, mainly. People collect that sort of thing. It's a specialised craft. Sometimes I do work for the odd regiment which wants a picture to hang in the mess. Famous battles and stuff. You know …"

"So you're not a disciple of the avant-garde. I might have guessed. Your hair's too short! Ha ha! No cubism or action painting, eh?" The Nigerian snapped the case back on his camera. "None of your 'which way up should I stand to look at it'?"

Karl laughed outright for the first time in ages. He was amused partly by the man's somewhat old-fashioned idea of the avant-garde, partly because he actually did paint stuff in his spare time which would fit the Nigerian's general description. All the same, he was pleased to have won the black man's approval.

"Not a revolutionary," said the man, stepping closer. "You're conventional, are you, in every respect?"

"Oh, hardly! Who is?"

"Who indeed? Have you had tea?" The black man took his arm, looking around him vaguely. "I understand there's a café here."

"A restaurant. On the other side."

"Shall we cross?"

"I don't know …" Karl shivered. He didn't much care for people holding him like that, particularly when they were strangers, but a touch shouldn't make him shiver. "I'm not sure …" Normally he could have walked away easily. Why should he mind being rude to a man who had so forcefully intruded on his privacy?

"You must have tea with me." The grip tightened just a little. "You have a bit of time to spare, surely? I rarely get the chance to make friends in London."

Now Karl felt guilty. He remembered his mother's advice. Good advice, for a change. "Never have anything to do with people who make you feel guilty". She should have

16

known! But it was no good. He did not want to disappoint the Nigerian. He felt rather faint suddenly. There was a sensation in the pit of his stomach which was not entirely unpleasurable.

They walked together through part of the Tudor Garden and through an archway which led into the Woodland Garden and there was the restaurant with its white wrought-iron tables and chairs on the veranda, its curve of glass through which the interior could be seen. The restaurant was quite busy today and was serving cucumber sandwiches and Danish pastries to little parties of women in jersey suits and silk frocks who were relaxing after their shopping. The only men present were one or two elderly husbands or fathers: tolerated because of their cheque-books. Karl and his new friend entered the restaurant and walked to the far end to a table by the window which looked out onto the lawns and willow trees skirting the miniature stream and its miniature wooden bridge. "You had better order, I think," said the Nigerian. "I'm not much used to this sort of thing." Again he smiled warmly. Karl picked up the menu.

"We might as well stick to the set tea," said Karl. "Sandwiches and cakes."

"Very well." The man's reply was vague, insouciant. He gave Karl the impression that, for all his politeness, he had weightier matters on his mind than the choice of food.

For a few moments Karl tried to signal a waitress. He felt embarrassed and avoided looking at his companion. He glanced about the crowded restaurant, at the pastel mauves and pinks and blues of the ladies suits, the fluffy hats built up layer on layer of artificial petals, The Jaeger scarves. At last the waitress arrived. He didn't know her. She was new. But she looked like the rest. A tired woman of about thirty-five. Her thin face was yellow beneath the powder, the rouge and the lipstick. She had bags under her eyes and the deep crow's feet emphasised the bleakness of her expression. The skin on the bridge of her nose was peeling. She had the hands of a hag twice her age. One of them plucked the order pad from where it hung by a string against her dowdy black skirt and she settled her pencil heavily against the paper. It seemed that she lacked even the strength to hold the stub with only one hand.

"Two set teas, please," said Karl. He tried to sound pleasant and sympathetic. But she paid attention neither to his face nor his tone.

"Thank you, sir." She let the pad fall back without using it. She began to trudge towards the kitchen, pushing open the door as if gratefully entering the gates of hell.

Karl felt the pressure of his companion's long legs against his own. He tried, politely, to move, but could not; not without a violent tug. The black man seemed unaware of Karl's discomfort and leaned forward over the little table, putting his two elbows on the dainty white cloth and looking directly into Karl's eyes. "I hope you don't think I've been rude, old chap," he said.

"Rude?" Karl was trapped by the eyes.

"It occurred to me you might have better things to do than keep a bored tourist entertained."

"Of course not," Karl heard himself say. "I'm afraid I don't know much about Nigeria. I'd like to know more. Of course, I followed the Biafran thing in the papers." Had that been the wrong remark?

"Your Alfred had similar trouble with his 'break-away' states, you know."

"I suppose he did." Karl wasn't sure who Alfred had been or what he had done.

The waitress came back with a mock-silver tray on which stood a teapot, a milk jug and a hot water jug, also of mock silver, together with cups and saucers and plates. She began to set her load down between the two men. The Nigerian leaned back but continued to smile into Karl's eyes while Karl murmured "Thank you" every time the waitress placed something in front of him. These ingratiating noises were his usual response to most minor forms of human misery, as they had been to his mother when she had made it evident what it had cost her to prepare a meal for him.

"Shall I be mother?" said Karl and again the not unpleasant sensation of weakness swept through him. The Nigerian was looking away, vague once again, his handsome

18

profile in silhouette as he took an interest in the garden. Karl repeated eagerly: "Shall I –?" The Nigerian said: "Fine." And Karl realised that he was now desperate to please his companion, that he needed the man's whole attention, that he would do anything to ensure that he got it. He poured the tea. He handed a cup to his friend, who accepted it absently.

"We haven't introduced ourselves," Karl said. He cleared his throat. "I'm Karl Glogauer."

The attention was regained. The eyes looked directly into Karl's, the pressure of the leg was deliberate. The Nigerian picked up the bowl nearest him and offered it to Karl.

"Sugar?"

"Thanks." Karl took the bowl.

"You've got nice hands," said the Nigerian. "An artist's hands, of course." Briefly, he touched Karl's fingers.

Karl giggled. "Do you think so?" The sensation came again, but this time it was a wave and there was no doubt about its origin. "Thank you." He smiled suddenly because to remark on their hands and to pretend to read their palms was one of his standard ways of trying to pick up girls. "Are you going to read my palm?"

The Nigerian's brows came together in a deep frown. "Why should I?"

Karl's breathing was heavier. At last he understood the nature of the trap. And there was nothing he wished to do about it.

In silence, they ate their sandwiches. Karl was no longer irritated by the pressure of the man's leg on his.

A little later the Nigerian said: "Will you come back with me?"

"Yes," whispered Karl.

He began to shake.

What Would You Do? (1)

You are a passenger on a plane which is about to crash. The plane is not a jet and so you have a chance to parachute to safety. With the other passengers, you stand in line and take one of the parachutes which the crew hands out to you. There is one problem. The people ahead of you on the line are already jumping out. But you have a four-month-old baby with you and it is too large to button into your clothing. Yet you must have both hands free in order to (a) pull the emergency ripcord in the event of the parachute failing to open, (b) guide the chute to safety if you see danger below. The baby is crying. The people behind you are pressing forward. Someone helps you struggle into the harness and hands you back your baby. Even if you did hold the baby in both hands and pray that you had an easy descent, there is every possibility he could be yanked from your grip as you jumped.

There are a few more seconds to go before you miss your chance to get out of the plane.

2

In The Commune: 1871: A Smile

Not only France, but the whole civilised world, was startled and dismayed by the sudden success of the Red Republicans of Paris. The most extraordinary, and perhaps the most alarming, feature of the movement, was the fact that it had been brought about by men nearly all of whom were totally unknown to society at large. It was not, therefore, the influence, whether for good or evil, of a few great names which might be supposed to exercise a species of enchantment on the uneducated classes, and to be capable of moving them, almost without thought, towards the execution of any design which the master-minds might have determined on – it was not this which had caused the convulsion. The outbreak was clearly due less to individual persuasion, which in the nature of things is evanescent, than to the operation of deep-rooted principles such as survive when men depart. The ideas which gave rise to the Commune were within the cognisance of the middle and upper classes of society; but it was not supposed that they had attained such power, or were capable of such organised action. A frightful apparition of the Red Republic had been momentarily visible in June, 1848; but it was at once exercised by the cannon and bayonets of Cavaignac. It was again apprehended towards the close of 1851, and would probably have made itself once more manifest, had not the coup d'etat of Louis Napoleon prevented any such movement, not only at that time, but for several years to come. Every now and then during the period of the Second Empire, threatenings of this vague yet appalling danger came and went, but the admirable organisation of the Imperial Government kept the enemies of social order in subjection, though only by a resort to means regrettable in themselves, against which the Moderate Republicans were perpetually directing their most bitter attacks, little thinking that they would soon be obliged to use the same weapons with still greater severity. Nevertheless, although the Emperor Napoleon held the Red Republic firmly down throughout his term of power, the principles of the extreme faction were working beneath the surface; and they only awaited the advent of a weaker Government, and of a period of social disruption, to glare upon the world with stormy menace.

HISTORY OF THE WAR BETWEEN FRANCE AND GERMANY
Anonymous.   *Cassell, Petter & Galpin, 1872.*

– *There you are, Karl.*
The black man strokes his head.
Karl has removed his clothes and lies naked on the double bed in the hotel suite. The silk counterpane is cool.
  – *Do you feel any better now?*
  – *I'm not sure.*
Karl's mouth is dry. The man's hands move down from his head to touch his shoulders. Karl gasps. He shuts his eyes.
Karl is seven years old. He and his mother have fled from their house as the Versaillais troops storm Paris in their successful effort to destroy the Commune established a few months earlier. It is civil war and it is savage. The more so, perhaps, because the French have received such an ignominious defeat at the hands of Bismarck's Prussians.
He is seven years old. It is the Spring of 1871. He is on the move.
  – *Do you like this? asks the black man.*

KARL WAS SEVEN. His mother was twenty-five. His father was thirty-one, but had probably been killed fighting the Prussians at St. Quentin. Karl's father had been so eager to join the National Guard and prove that he was a true Frenchman.

"Now, Karl." His mother put him down and he felt the hard cobbles of the street beneath his thin shoes. "You must walk a little. Mother is tired, too."

It was true. When she was tired, her Alsatian accent always became thicker and now it was very thick. Karl felt ashamed for her.

He was not sure what was happening. The previous night he had heard loud noises and the sounds of running feet. There had been shots and explosions, but such things were familiar enough since the Siege of Paris. Then his mother had appeared in her street clothes and made him put on his coat and shoes, hurrying him from the room and down the stairs and into the street. He wondered what had happened to their maid. When they got into the street he saw that a fire had broken out some distance away and that there were many National Guardsmen about. Some of them were running towards the fires and others, who were wounded, were staggering in the other direction. Some bad soldiers were attacking them, he gathered, and his mother was afraid that the house would be burned down. "Starvation – bombardment – and now fire," she had muttered bitterly. "I hope all the wretched Communards are shot!" Her heavy black skirts hissed as she led him through the night, away from the fighting.

By dawn, more of the city was burning and all was confusion. Ragged members of the National Guard in their stained uniforms rallied the citizens to pile furniture and bedding onto the carts which had been overturned to block the streets. Sometimes Karl and his mother were stopped and told to help the other women and children, but she gave excuses and hurried on. Karl was dazed. He had no idea where they were going. He was vaguely aware that his mother knew no better than he. When he gasped that he could walk no further, she picked him up and continued her flight, her sharp face expressing her disapproval at his weakness. She was a small, wiry woman who would have been reasonably pretty had her features not been set so solidly in a mask of tension and anxiety. Karl had never known her face to soften, either to him or to his father. Her eyes had always seemed fixed on some distant objective which, secretly and grimly, she had determined to reach. That same look was in her eyes now, though much more emphatic, and the little boy had the impression that his mother's flight through the city was the natural climax to her life.

Karl tried not to cry out as he trotted behind his mother's dusty black skirts. His whole body was aching and his feet were blistered and once he fell on the cobbles and had to scramble up swiftly in order to catch her as she turned a corner.

They were now in a narrow side street not far from the Rue du Bac on the Left Bank. Twice Karl had caught a glimpse of the nearby Seine. It was a beautiful spring morning, but the sky was slowly being obscured by thick smoke from the many burning buildings on both sides of the river. Noticing this, his mother hesitated.

"Oh, the animals!" Her tone was a mixture of disgust and despair. "They are setting fire to their own city!"

"May we rest now, mother?" asked Karl.

"Rest?" She laughed bitterly. But she made no effort to continue on her way, though she cast about her in every direction, trying to decide where she could best expect to find safety.

Suddenly, from a couple of streets away, there came a series of explosions which shook the houses. There were shots and then a great angry cry, followed by individual screams and shouts. In the guise of addressing her son, she muttered to herself.

"The streets are not safe. The dogs are everywhere. We must try to find some government soldiers and ask their protection."

"Are those the bad soldiers, mother?"

"No, Karl, they are the good soldiers. They are freeing

Paris of those who have brought the city to ruin."

"The Prussians?"

"The Communists. We all knew it would come to this. What a fool your father was."

Karl was surprised to hear the contempt in her voice. She had previously always told him to look up to his father. He began to cry. For the first time since leaving the house, he felt deeply miserable, rather than merely uncomfortable.

"Oh, my God!" His mother reached out and shook him. "We don't need your weeping on top of everything else. Be quiet, Karl."

He bit his lip, but he was still shaken by sobs.

She stroked his head. "Your mother is tired," she said. "She has always done her duty." A sigh. "But what's the point?" Karl realised that she was not trying to comfort him at all, but herself. Even the automatic stroking of his hair was done in an effort to calm herself. There was no real sympathy in the gesture. For some reason this knowledge made him feel deep sympathy for her. It has not been easy, even when his father was alive, with no-one coming to buy clothes in the shop just because they had a German-sounding name. And she had protected him from the worst of the insults and beaten the boys who threw stones at him.

He hugged her waist. "Have courage, mother," he whispered awkwardly.

She looked at him in astonishment. "Courage? What does it gain us?" She took his hand. "Come. We'll find the soldiers."

Trotting beside her, Karl felt closer to her than he had ever felt, not because she had shown affection for him but because he had been able to show affection for her. Of late, he had begun to feel guilty, believing he might not love his mother as much as a good son should.

The two of them entered the somewhat broader street that was Rue du Bac and here was the source of the sounds they had heard. The Communards were being beaten back by the well-trained Versailles troops. The Versaillese, having been so roundly defeated by the Prussians, were avenging themselves on their recalcitrant countrymen. Most of the Communards were armed with rifles on which were fixed bayonets. They had run out of ammunition and were using the rifles as spears. Most of them were dressed in ordinary clothes, but there was a handful of National Guardsmen among them, in soiled pale blue uniforms. Karl saw a torn red flag still flying somewhere. Many women were taking part in the fighting. Karl saw one woman bayonet a wounded Versaillese who lay on the ground. His mother pulled him away. She was trembling now. As they rounded a bend in the Rue du Bac, they saw another barricade. Then there was an eruption and a roar and the barricades flew apart. Through the dust and debris Karl saw bodies flung in every direction. Some of the dead were children of his own age. A terrifying wailing filled the street, a wailing which turned into a growl of anger. The remaining Communards began to fire at the unseen enemy. Another eruption and another roar and the remains of the barricade went down. For a second there was silence. Then a woman rushed from a nearby house and screamed something, hurling a burning bottle through an open window in her own cellar. Karl saw that a house on the opposite side of the street was beginning to burn. Why were the people setting fire to their own houses?

Now through the smoke and the ruins came the Versaillese in their smart dark blue and red uniforms. Their eyes were red and glaring, reflecting the flames. They frightened Karl far more than the National Guardsmen. Behind them galloped an officer on a black horse. He was screaming in the same high-pitched tone as the woman. He was waving a sabre. Karl's mother took a step towards the troops and then hesitated. She turned and began to run in the other direction, Karl running with her.

There were several shots and Karl noticed that bullets were striking the walls of the houses. He knew at once that he and his mother were being fired at. He grinned with excitement.

They dashed down the next sidestreet and had to wade through piles of garbage to enter a ruined building, an earlier victim of the first Siege. His mother hid behind a quaking wall as the soldiers ran past. When they had gone she sat down on a slab of broken stone and began to cry. Karl stroked her hair, wishing that he could share her grief.

"Your father should not have deserted us," she said.

"He had to fight, mother," said Karl. It was what she had said to him when his father joined the Guard. "For France."

"For the Reds. For the fools who brought all this upon us!"

Karl did not understand.

Soon his mother was sleeping in the ruins. He curled up beside her and slept, too.

When they awakened that afternoon there was much more smoke. It drifted everywhere. On all sides buildings burned. Karl's mother staggered up. Without looking at him or speaking to him, she seized his hand in a grip which made him wince. Her boots slipping on the stones, her skirts all filthy and ragged at the hem, she dragged him with her to the street. A young girl stood there, her face grave. "Good day," she said.

"Are they still fighting?"

The girl could hardly understand his mother's accent, it had become so thick. The girl frowned.

"Are they still fighting?" his mother asked again, speaking in a peculiar, slow voice.

"Yes." The girl shrugged. "They are killing everyone. Anyone."

"That way?" Karl's mother pointed towards the Seine. "That way?"

"Yes. Everywhere. But more that way." She pointed in the general direction of the Boulevard du Montparnasse. "Are you a petrol-woman?"

"Certainly not!" Madame Glogauer glared at the girl. "Are you?"

"I wasn't allowed," said the girl regretfully. "There isn't much petrol left."

Karl's mother took him back the way they had come. The fires which had been started earlier were now out. It appeared that they had done little damage. Not enough petrol, thought Karl.

With her sleeve over her mouth, his mother picked her way through the corpses and crossed the ruins of the barricade. The other men and women who were searching for dead friends or relatives ignored them as they went by.

Karl thought there were more dead people than living people in the world now.

They reached the Boulevard St.-Germaine, hurrying towards the Quai d'Orsay. On the far side of the river monstrous sheets of flame sprang from a dozen buildings and smoke boiled into the clear May sky.

"I am so thirsty, mother," murmured Karl. The smoke and the dust filled his mouth. She ignored him.

Here again the barricades were deserted, save for the dead, the victors and the sightseers. Groups of Versaillese stood about, leaning on their rifles, smoking and watching the fires, or chatting to the innocent citizens who were so anxious to establish their hatred of the Communards. Karl saw a group of prisoners, their hands bound with rope, sitting miserably in the road, guarded by the regular soldiers. Whenever a Communard moved, he would receive a harsh blow from a rifle butt or would be threatened by the bayonet. The red flag flew nowhere. In the distance came the sound of cannon fire and rifle fire.

"At last!" Madame Glogauer began to move towards the troops. "We shall go home soon, Karl. If they have not burned our house down."

Karl saw an empty wine bottle in the gutter. Perhaps they could fill it with water from the river. He picked it up even as his mother dragged him forward.

"Mother – we could . . ."

She stopped. "What have you got there? Put the filthy thing down!"

"We could fill it with water."

"We'll drink soon enough. And eat."

She grabbed the bottle from his hand. "If we are to remain respectable, Karl . . ."

She turned her head at a shout. A group of citizens were pointing at her. Soldiers began to run towards them. Karl heard the word "petroleuse" repeated several times. Madame Glogauer shook her head and threw the bottle down. "It is empty," she said quietly. They could not hear her. The soldiers stopped and raised their rifles She stretched her hands towards them. "It was an empty bottle!" she cried.

Karl tugged at her. "Mother!" He tried to take her hand, but it was still stretched towards the soldiers. "They cannot understand you, mother."

She began to back away and then she ran. He tried to follow, but fell down. She disappeared into a little alley. The soldiers ran past Karl and followed her into the alley. The citizens ran after the soldiers. They were shrieking with hysteria and bloodlust. Karl got up and ran behind them. There were some shots and some screams. By the time Karl had entered the little street the soldiers were coming back again, the citizens still standing looking at something on the ground. Karl pushed his way through them. They cuffed him and snarled at him and then they, too, turned away.

"The pigs use women and children to fight their battles," said one man. He glared at Karl. "The sooner Paris is cleansed of such scum the better."

His mother lay sprawled on her face in the filth of the street. There was a dark, wet patch on her back. Karl went up to her and, as he had suspected, found that the patch was blood. She was still bleeding. He had never seen his mother's blood before. He tried hard to turn her over, but he was too weak. "Mother?" Suddenly her whole body heaved and she drew in a great dry breath. Then she moaned.

The smoke drifted across the sky and evening came and the city burned. Red flames stained the night on every side. Shots boomed. But there were no more voices. Even the people who passed and whom Karl begged to help his wounded mother did not speak. One or two laughed harshly. With his help, his mother managed to turn herself over and sat with her back propped against the wall. She breathed with great difficulty and did not seem to know him, staring as fixedly and as determinedly into the middle distance as she had always done. Her hair was loose and it clung to her tight, anxious face. Karl wanted to find her some water, but he did not want to leave her.

At last he got up and blocked the path of a man who came walking towards Boulevard St-Germaine. "Please help my mother, sir," he said.

"Help her? Yes, of course. Then they will shoot me, too. That will be good, eh?" The man threw back his head and laughed heartily as he continued on his way.

"She did nothing wrong!" Karl shouted.

The man stopped just before he turned the corner. "It depends how you look at it, doesn't it, young man?" He gestured into the boulevard. "Here's what you need! Hey, there! Stop! I've got another passenger for you." Karl heard the sound of something squeaking. The squeaking stopped and the man exchanged a few words with someone else. Then he disappeared. Instinctively Karl backed away with some idea of defending his mother. A filthy old man appeared next. "I've just about got room," he complained. He brushed Karl aside, heaved Madame Glogauer onto his shoulder and turned, staggering back down the street. Karl followed. Was the man going to help his mother? Take her to the hospital?

A cart stood in the street. There were no cart-horses, for they had all been eaten during the Siege as Karl knew. Instead, between the shafts stood several ragged men and women. They began to move forward when they saw the old man appear again, dragging the squeaking cart behind them. Karl saw that there were people of all ages and sexes lying on top of one another in the cart. Most of them were dead, many with gaping wounds and parts of their faces or bodies missing. "Give us a hand here," said the old man and one of the younger men left his place at the front and helped heave Madame Glogauer onto the top of the pile. She groaned.

"Where are you taking her?" asked Karl.

They continued to ignore him. The cart squeaked on through the night. Karl followed it. From time to time he heard his mother moan.

He became very tired and could hardly see, for his eyes

30

kept closing, but he followed the cart by its sound, hearing the sharp clack of clogs and the slap of bare feet on the road, the squeal of the wheels, the occasional cries and moans of the living passengers. By midnight they had reached one of the outlying districts of the city and entered a square. There were Versaillese soldiers here, standing about on the remains of a green. In the middle of the green was a dark area. The old man said something to the soldiers and then he and his companions began unloading the cart. Karl tried to see which one of the people was his mother. The ragged men and women carried their burdens to the dark area and dropped them into it. Karl could now see that it was a freshly dug pit. There were already a large number of bodies in it. He peered in, certain that he had heard his mother's voice among the moans of the wounded as, indiscriminately, they were buried with the dead. All around the square shutters were closing and lights were being extinguished. A soldier came up and dragged Karl away from the graveside. "Get back," he said, "or you'll go in with them."

Soon the cart went away. The soldiers sat down by the graveside and lit their pipes, complaining about the smell, which had become almost overpowering, and passing a bottle of wine back and forth. "I'll be glad when this is over," said one.

Karl squatted against the wall of the house, trying to distinguish his mother's voice amongst those which groaned or cried out from the pit. He was sure he could hear her pleading to be let out.

By dawn, her voice had stopped and the cart came back with a fresh load. These were dumped into the pit and the soldiers got up reluctantly at the command of their officer, putting down their rifles and picking up shovels. They began to throw earth onto the bodies.

When the grave was covered, Karl got up and began to walk away.

The guards put down their shovels. They seemed more cheerful now and they opened another bottle of wine. One of them saw Karl. "Hello, young man. You're up early." He ruffled the boy's hair. "Hoping for some more excitement, eh?" He took a pull on the bottle and then offered it to Karl. "Like a drink?" He laughed.

Karl smiled at him.

Karl gasps and he writhes on the bed.
– What are you doing? he says.
– Don't you like it? You don't have to like it. Not everyone does.
– Oh, God, says Karl.
The black man gets up. His body gleams in the faint light from the window. He moves gracefully back, out of range of Karl's vision. – Perhaps you had better sleep. There is lots of time.
– No ...
– You want to go on?
A pause.
– Yes ...

What Would You Do? (2)

You have been brought to a room by the Secret Police.

They say that you can save the lives of your whole family if you will only assist them in one way.

You agree to help.

There is a table covered by a cloth. They remove the cloth and reveal a profusion of objects. There is a children's comforter, a Smith and Wesson .45, an umbrella, a big volume of Don Quixote, illustrated by Doré, two blankets, a jar of honey, four bottles of drugs, a bicycle pump, some blank envelopes, a carton of Sullivans cigarettes, an enamelled pin with the word 1900 on it (blue on gold), a wrist-watch, a Japanese fan.

They tell you that all you have to do is choose the correct object and you and your family will be released.

You have never seen any of the objects before. You tell them this. They nod. That is all right. They know. Now choose.

You stare at the objects, trying to divine their significance.

3

Kaffee Klatsch in Brunswick: 1883: The Lowdown

Bismarck was very fond of enlarging on his favourite theory of the male and female European nations. The Germans themselves, the three Scandinavian peoples, the Dutch, the English proper, the Scotch, the Hungarians and the Turks, he declared to be essentially male races. The Russians, the Poles, the Bohemians, and indeed every Slavonic people, and all Celts, he maintained, just as emphatically, to be female races. A female race he ungallantly defined as one given to immense verbosity, to fickleness, and to lack of tenacity. He conceded to these feminine races some of the advantages of their sex, and acknowledged that they had great powers of attraction and charm, when they chose to exert them, and also a fluency of speech denied to the more virile nations. He maintained stoutly that it was quite useless to expect efficiency in any form from one of the female races, and he was full of contempt for the Celt and the Slav. He contended that the most interesting nations were the epicene ones, partaking, that is, of the characteristics of both sexes, and he instanced France and Italy, intensely virile in the North, absolutely female in the South; maintaining that the Northern French had saved their country times out of number from the follies of the "Meridionaux". He attributed the efficiency of the Frenchmen of the North to the fact that they had so large a proportion of Frankish and Norman blood in their veins, the Franks being a Germanic tribe, and the Normans, as their name implied, Northmen of Scandinavian, therefore also of Teutonic, origin. He declared that the fair-haired Piedmontese were the driving power of Italy, and that they owed their initiative to their descent from the Germanic hordes who invaded Italy under Alaric in the fifth century. Bismarck stoutly maintained that efficiency wherever it was found, was due to Teutonic blood; a statement with which I will not quarrel.

As the inventor of "Practical Politics" (*Real-Politik*), Bismarck had a supreme contempt for fluent talkers and for words, saying that only fools could imagine that facts could be talked away. He cynically added that words were sometimes useful for "papering over structural cracks" when they had to be concealed for a time.

With his intensely overbearing disposition, Bismarck could not brook the smallest contradiction, or any criticism whatever. I have often watched him in the Reichstag – then housed in a very modest building – whilst being attacked, especially by Liebknecht the Socialist. He made no effort to conceal his anger, and would stab the blotting-pad before him viciously with a metal paper-cutter, his face purple with rage.

Bismarck himself was a very clear and forcible speaker, with a happy knack of coining felicitous phrases.

THE VANISHED POMPS OF YESTERDAY.
Lord Frederick Hamilton.
Hodder and Stoughton, 1920.

There is a big colour TV in the suite.

The Nigerian walks up to it. His penis is still slightly stiff. – Do you want this on?

Karl is eight. It is 1883. Brunswick. He has a very respectable mother and father. They are kind but firm. It is very comfortable.

He shakes his head.

– Well, do you mind if I watch the news?

Karl is eight. It is 1948. There is a man in pyjamas in his mother's room.

It is 1883 . . .

KARL WAS EIGHT. His mother was thirty-five. His father was forty. They had a large, modern house in the best part of Brunswick. His father's business was in the centre of town. Trade was good in Germany and particularly good in Brunswick. The Glogauers were part of the best society in Brunswick. Frau Glogauer belonged to the coffee circle which once a week met, in rotation, at the house of one of the members. This week the ladies were meeting at Frau Glogauer's.

Karl, of course, was not allowed into the big drawing room where his mother entertained. His nurse watched over him while he played in the garden in the hot summer sunshine. Through the french windows, which were open, he could just see his mother and her friends. They balanced the delicate china cups so elegantly and they leaned their heads so close together when they talked. They were not bored. Karl was bored.

He swung back and forth on his swing. Up and down and back and forward and up and down and back. He was dressed in his best velvet suit and he was hot and uncomfortable. But he always dressed in this way when it was his mother's turn to entertain the kaffee-klatsch, even though he wasn't invited to join them. Usually he was asked to come in just before the ladies left. They would ask him the same questions as they asked every time and they would compliment his mother on his looks and his size and his health and they would give him a little piece of gateau. He was looking forward to the gateaux.

"Karl, you must wear your hat," said Miss Henshaw. Miss Henshaw was English and her German was rather unfortunate in that she had learned it in a village. It was Low German and it made her sound like a yokel. Karl's parents and their friends spoke nothing but the more sophisticated High German. Low German sounded just like English, anyway. He didn't know why she'd bothered to learn it. "Your hat, Karl. The sun is too hot."

In her garishly striped blouse and her silly, stiff grey skirt and her own floppy white hat, Miss Henshaw looked awful. How dowdy and decrepit she was compared to Mother who, corsetted and bustled and covered in pretty silk ribbons and buttons and lace and brocade, moved with the dignity of a six-masted clipper. Miss Henshaw was evidently only a servant, for all her pretense at authority.

She stretched out her freckled arm, offering him the little sun hat. He ignored her, making the swing go higher and higher.

"You will get sunstroke, Karl. Your mother will be very angry with me."

Karl shrugged and kicked his feet out straight, enjoying Miss Henshaw's helplessness.

"Karl! Karl!"

Miss Henshaw's voice was almost a screech.

Karl grinned. He saw that the ladies were looking out at him through the open window. He waved to his mother. The ladies smiled and returned to their gossip.

He knew it was gossip, about everyone in Brunswick, because once he had lain beside the window in the shrubs and listened before he had been caught by Miss Henshaw. He wished that he had understood more of the references, but at least he had got one useful tip – that Fritz Vieweg's father had been born "the wrong side of the blanket". He hadn't been sure of the meaning, but when he had confronted Fritz Vieweg with it, it had stopped Vieweg calling him a "Jew-pig" all right.

Gossip like that was worth a lot.

"Karl! Karl!"

"Oh, go away Fraulein Henshaw. I am not in need of my hat at present." He chuckled to himself. When he talked like his father, she always disapproved.

His mother appeared in the doorway of the french window.

"Karl, dear. There is someone who would like to meet

you. May we have Karl in with us for a moment, Miss Henshaw?"

"Of course, Frau Glogauer." Miss Henshaw darted him a look of stern triumph. Reluctantly, he let the swing slow down and then jumped off.

Miss Henshaw took his hand and they walked across the ornamental pavement to the french windows. His mother smiled fondly and patted his head.

"Frau Spiegelberg is here and wants to meet you."

He supposed, from his mother's tone, that he should know who Frau Spiegelberg was, that she must be an important visitor, not one of Frau Glogauer's regulars. A woman dressed in purple and white silk was towering behind his mother. She gave him quite a friendly smile. He bowed twice very deeply. "Good afternoon, Frau Spiegelberg."

"Good afternoon, Karl," said Frau Spiegelberg.

"Frau Spiegelberg is from Berlin, Karl," said his mother. "She has met the great Chancellor Bismarck himself!"

Again Karl bowed.

The ladies laughed. Frau Spiegelberg said with charming, almost coquettish modesty, "I must emphasise I am not on intimate terms with Prinz Bismarck!" and she gave a trilling laugh. Karl knew that all the ladies would be practising that laugh after she had gone back to Berlin.

"I would like to go to Berlin," said Karl.

"It is a very fine city," said Frau Spiegelberg complacently. "But your Brunswick is very pretty."

Karl was at a loss for something to say. He frowned and then brightened. "Frau Spiegelberg –" he gave another little bow – "have you met Chancellor Bismarck's son?"

"I have met both. Do you mean Herbert or William or –" Frau Spiegelberg glanced modestly at her companions again – "Bill as he likes to be called."

"Bill," said Karl.

"I have attended several balls at which he has been present, yes."

"So you – have touched him, Frau Spiegelberg?"

And again the trilling laugh. "Why do you ask?"

"Well, Father met him once I believe when on business in Berlin..."

"So your Father and I have an acquaintance in common. That is splendid, Karl." Frau Spiegelberg made to turn away, "A handsome boy, Frau –"

"And Father shook hands with him," said Karl.

"Really? Well..."

"And Father said he drank so much beer that his hands were always wet and clammy and he could not possibly live for long if he continued to drink that much. Father is, himself, not averse to a few tots of beer or glasses of punch, but he swears he has never seen anyone drink so much in all his life. Is Bill Bismarck dead yet, Frau Spiegelberg?"

His mother had been listening to him in cold horror, her mouth open. Frau Spiegelberg raised her eyebrows. The other ladies glanced at each other. Miss Henshaw took his hand and began to pull him away, apologising to his mother.

Karl bowed again. "I am honoured to have met you, Frau Spiegelberg," he said in his father's voice. "I am afraid I have embarrassed you and so I will take my leave now." Miss Henshaw's tugging became more insistent. "I hope we shall meet again before you return to Berlin, Frau Spiegelberg..."

"It is time I left," icily said Frau Spiegelberg to his mother.

His mother came out for a moment and hissed:

"You disgusting child. You will be punished for this. Your father shall do it."

"But, Mother..."

"In the meantime, Miss Henshaw," said Frau Glogauer in a terrible murmur, "you have my permission to beat the boy."

Karl shuddered as he caught a glint of hidden malice in Miss Henshaw's pale, grey eyes.

"Very well, madame," said Miss Henshaw. As she led him away he heard her sigh a deep sigh of pleasure.

Already, he was plotting his own revenge.

– You'll like it better when you get used to it. It's a question of your frame of mind.

Karl sighs. – Maybe.

– It's a matter of time, that's all.

– I believe you.

– You've got to let yourself go.

They sip the dry, chilled champagne the black man has ordered. Outside, people are going into the theatres.

– After all, says the black man – we are many people. There are a lot of different sides to one's personality. You musn't feel that you've lost something. You have gained something. Another aspect is flowering.

– I feel terrible.

– It won't last. Your moment will come.

Karl smiles. The black man's English is not always perfect.

– There, you see, you are feeling more relaxed already. The black man reaches out and touches his arm. – How smooth your flesh is. What are you thinking?

– I was remembering the time I found the air-raid warden in bed with my mother. I remember her explaining it to my father. My father was a patient man.

– Is your father still alive?

– I don't know.

– You have a great deal to learn, yet.

What Would You Do? (3)

You are returning from the theatre after a pleasant evening with your sweetheart. You are in the centre of the city and you want a taxi. You decide to go to the main railway station and find a taxi there. As you come into a side-entrance and approach a flight of steps you see an old man trying to ascend. He is evidently incapably drunk. Normally you would help him up the steps, but in this case there is a problem. His trousers have fallen down to his ankles, revealing his filthy legs. From his bottom protrude several pieces of newspaper covered in excrement. To help him would be a messy task, to say the least, and you are reluctant to spoil the previously pleasant mood of the evening. There is a second or two before you pass him and continue on your journey.

4

Capetown Party:
1892: Butterflies

In the meantime let us not forget that if errors of
judgement have been committed, they have been
committed by men whose zeal and patriotism has
never been doubted. We cannot refrain, however,
from alluding here to the greatest of all lessons
which this war has taught, not us alone, but all the
world – the solidarity of the Empire. And for that
great demonstration what sacrifice was not worth
making.

WITH THE FLAG TO PRETORIA.
H. W. Wilson, Harmsworth Brothers 1900.

*Karl emerges from the deep bath. Liquid drips from him.
He stares in bewilderment at himself in the wall mirror op-
posite.*
   – Why did you make me do that?
   *– I thought you'd like it. You said how much you ad-
mired my body.*
   – I meant your physique.
   – Oh, I see.
   *– I look like something out of a minstrel show. Al Jol-
son . . .*

– Yes, you do rather. But you could pass for what? An
Eurasian? The black man begins to laugh.
Karl laughs, too.
They fall into each other's arms.
– It shouldn't take long to dry, says the black man.
Karl is nine. Is is 1892. He is at work now.
– I think I like you better like that, says the black man.
He puts a palm on Karl's damp thigh. – It's your colour ...
Karl giggles.
– There, you see, it has made you feel better.

KARL WAS NINE. His mother did not know her age. He did
not know his father. He was a servant in a house with a
huge garden. A white house. He was the punkah-wallah,
the boy who operated the giant fan which swept back and
forth over the white people while they were eating. When he
was not doing this, he helped the cook in the kitchen. Whenever he could, however, he was out in the grounds with his
net. He had a passion for butterflies. He had a large collection in the room he shared with the two other little houseboys and his companions were very envious. If he saw a
specimen he did not own, he would forget everything else
until he had caught it. Everyone knew about his hobby and
that was why he was known as "Butterfly" by everyone,
from the master and mistress down. It was a kind house
and they tolerated his passion. It was not everyone, even,
who would employ a Cape Coloured boy, because most
thought that halfbreeds were less trustworthy than pure-
blooded natives. The master had presented him with a
proper killing jar and an old velvet-lined case in which to
mount his specimens. Karl was very lucky.

Whenever the master saw him, he would say: "And
how's the young entomologist, today?" and Karl would
flash him a smile. When Karl was older it was almost certain that he would be given a position as a footman. He
would be the very first Cape Coloured footman in this district.

This evening it was very hot and the master and mistress
were entertaining a large party of guests to dinner. Karl sat

behind a screen and pulled on the string which made the fan work. He was good at his job and the motion of the fan was as regular as the swinging of a pendulum.

When his right arm became tired, Karl would use his left arm, and when his left arm was tired, he would transfer the string to the big toe of his right foot. When his right foot ached, he would use his left and by that time his right arm would be rested and he could begin again. In the meantime, he daydreamed, thinking of his lovely butterflies and of the specimens he had yet to collect. There was a very large one he wanted particularly. It had blue and yellow wings and a complicated pattern of zigzags on its body. He did not know its name. He knew few of the names because nobody could tell them to him. Someone had once shown him a book with some pictures of butterflies and the names underneath, but since he could not read he could not discover what the names were.

Laughter came from the other side of the screen. A deep voice said: "Somebody will teach the Boers a lesson soon, mark my words. Those damned farmers can't go on treating British subjects in that high-handed fashion forever. We've made their country rich and they treat us like natives!"

Another voice murmured a reply and the deep voice said loudly: "If that's the sort of life they want to preserve, why don't they go somewhere else? They've got to move with the times."

Karl lost interest in the conversation. He didn't understand it, anyway. Besides, he was more interested in butterflies. He transferred the string to his left toe.

When all the guests had withdrawn, a footman came to tell Karl that he might go to his supper. Stiffly Karl walked round the screen and hobbled towards the door. The dinner had been a long one.

In the kitchen the cook put a large plate of succulent scraps before him and said: "Hurry up now, young man. I've had a long day and I want to get to my bed."

He ate the food and washed it down with the half a glass of beer the cook gave him. It was a treat. She knew he had been working hard, too. As she let him out of the kitchen, she rumpled his hair and said: "Poor little chap. How's your butterflies?"

"Very well, thank you, cook." Karl was always polite. "You must show them to me sometime."

"I'll show them to you tomorrow, if you like."

She nodded. "Well, sometime ... Goodnight, Butterfly."

"Goodnight, cook."

He climbed the back stairs high up to his room in the roof. The two houseboys were already asleep. Quietly, he lit his lamp and got out his case of butterflies. He would be needing another case soon.

Smiling tenderly, he delicately stroked their wings with the tip of his little finger.

For over an hour he looked at his butterflies and then he got into his bed and pulled the sheet over him. He lay staring at the eaves and thinking about the blue and yellow butterfly he would try to catch tomorrow.

There was a sound outside. He ignored it. It was a familiar sound. Feet creeping along the passage. Either one of the housemaids was on her way out to keep an assignation with her follower, or her follower had boldly entered the house. Karl turned over and tried to go to sleep.

The door of his room opened.

He turned onto his back again and peered through the gloom. A white figure was standing there, panting. It was a man in pyjamas and a dressing gown. The man paused for a moment and then crept towards Karl's bed.

"There you are, you little beauty," whispered the man. Karl recognised the voice as the one he had heard earlier talking about the Boers.

"What do you want, sir?" Karl sat up in bed.

"Eh? Damn! Who the devil are you?"

"The punkah-boy, sir."

"I thought this was where that little fat maid slept. What the devil!"

There was a crunch and the man grunted in pain, hopping about the room. "Oh, I've had enough of this!"

Now the other two boys were awake. Their eyes stared in

horror at the hopping figure. Perhaps they thought it was a ghost.

The white man blundered back out of the room, leaving the door swinging on its hinges. Karl heard him go down the passage and descend the stairs.

Karl got up and lit the lamp.

He saw his butterfly case where he had left it beside the bed. The white man had stepped on it and broken the glass. All the butterflies were broken, too.

– *Won't it wash off? asks Karl.*
– *Do you want it to come off? Don't you feel more free?*
– *Free?*

What Would You Do? (4)

You are escaping from an enemy. You have climbed along the top of a sloping slate roof, several storeys up. It is raining. You slip and manage to hang on to the top of the roof. You try to get back, but your feet slip on the wet tiles. Below you, you can see a lead gutter. Will you risk sliding down the roof while there is still some strength left in your fingers and hope that you can catch the gutter as you go down and thus work your way to safety? Or will you continue to try to pull yourself back to the top of the roof? There is also the chance that the gutter will break under your weight when you grab it. Perhaps, also, your enemy has discovered where you are and is coming along the roof towards you.

5

Liberation in Havana:
1898: Hooks

"You may fire when ready, Gridley."

COMMODORE DEWEY, *May 1st, 1898.*

– *There, it's dried nicely. The black man runs his nail down Karl's chest.* – *Are you religious, Karl?*
– *Not really.*
– *Do you belive in incarnation? Or what you might call "transincarnation", I suppose.*
– *I don't know what you're talking about.*
The nail traces a line across his stomach. He gasps.
The black man bares his teeth in a sudden smile.
– *Oh, you do really. What's this? Wilful ignorance? How many people today suffer from that malaise!*
– *Leave me alone.*
– *Alone?*
Karl is ten, the son of a small manufacturer of cigars in Havana, Cuba. His grandfather had the cigar factory before his father. He will inherit the factory from his father.
– *Yes – alone . . . Oh, God!*
. . . The black man's tone becomes warmly sympathetic. What's up?
Karl looks at him in surprise, hearing him speak English slang easily for the first time. The black man is changing.
Karl shudders. – *You've – you've – made me cold . . .*

– Then we'd better tuck you into bed, old chap.

– You've corrupted me.

– Corrupted? Is that what you think turns me on? The Corruption of Ignorance! The black man throws back his handsome head and laughs heartily.

Karl is ten . . .

The black man leans down and kisses Karl ferociously on the lips.

KARL WAS TEN. His mother was dead. His father was fifty one. His brother Willi was nineteen and, when last heard of, had joined the insurgents to fight against the Spaniards.

Karl's father had not approved of Willi's decision and had disowned his eldest son; that was why Karl was now the heir to the cigar factory. One day he would be master of nearly a hundred women and children who worked in the factory rolling the good cigars which were prized all over the world.

Not that business could be said to be good at present, with the American ships blockading the port. "But the war is virtually over," said Senor Glogauer, "and things will be returning to normal soon enough."

It was Sunday and the bells were ringing all over Havana. Big bells and little bells. It was almost impossible to hear anything else.

After church, Senor Glogauer walked with his son down the Prado towards Parque Central. Since the war, the beggars seemed to have multiplied to four or five times their previous number. Disdaining a carriage, Senor Glogauer led his son through the ragged clamourers, tapping a way through with his cane. Sometimes a particularly sluggish beggar would receive a heavy thwack for his pains and Senor Glogauer would smile to himself and put a little extra tilt on his beautifully white Panama hat. His suit was white, too. Karl wore a coffee-coloured sailor suit and sweated. His father made a point of making this journey on foot every Sunday because he said Karl must learn to know the people and not fear them; they were all wretched cowards, even when you had to deal with a whole pack of them, as now.

This morning a brigade of volunteers had been lined up for inspection in the Prado. Their uniforms were ill-fitting and not all of them had rifles of the same make, but a little Spanish lieutenant strutted up and down in front of them as proudly as if he were Napoleon inspecting the Grand Army. And behind the marshalled volunteers a military band played rousing marches and patriotic tunes. The bells and the beggars and the band created such a cacaphony that Karl felt his ears would close up against the noise. It echoed through the faded white grandeur of the street, from the elaborate stucco walls of the hotels and official buildings on both sides of the avenue, from the black and shining windows of the shops with their ornate gold, silver and scarlet lettering. And mingled with this noise were the smells – smells from sewers and beggars and sweating soldiers threatening to drown the more savoury smells of coffee and candy and cooking food.

Karl was glad when they entered the babble of the Café Inglaterra on the west side of the Parque Central. This was the fashionable place to come and, as always, it was crowded with the representatives of all nations, professions and trades. There were Spanish officers, businessmen, lawyers, priests. There were a number of ladies in colours as rich as the feathers of the jungle birds (from whom they had borrowed at least part of their finery), there were merchants from all the countries of Europe. There were English planters and even a few American journalists or tobacco-buyers. They sat at the tables, crowded tightly together, and drank beer or punch or whisky, talking, laughing, quarrelling. Some stood at the counters while upstairs others ate late breakfasts or early luncheons or merely drank coffee.

Senor Glogauer guided Karl into the cafe, nodding to acquaintances, smiling at friends, and found a seat for himself. "You had better stand, Karl, until a seat becomes free," he said. "Your usual lemonade?"

"Thank you, Papa." Karl wished he could be at home reading his book in the cool semi-darkness of the nursery.

Senor Glogauer studied the menu. "The cost!" he exclaimed. "I'll swear it has doubled since last week."

The man sitting opposite spoke good Spanish but was evidently English or American. He smiled at Senor Glogauer. "It's true what you people say – you're not being blockaded by the warships. You're being blockaded by the grocers!"

Senor Glogauer pursed his lips in a cautious smile. "Our own people are ruining us, senor. You are quite right. The tradesmen are soaking the life out of us. They blame the Americans, but I know they had prepared for this – salting away their food knowing that if the blockade took effect they could charge anything they liked. It is hard for us at the moment, senor."

"So I see," said the stranger wryly. "When the Americans get here things will be better, eh?"

Senor Glogauer shrugged. "Not if La Lucha is correct. I was reading yesterday of the atrocities the American Rough Riders are committing in Santiago. They are drunk all the time. They steal. They shoot honest citizens at will – and worse." Senor Glogauer glanced significantly at Karl. The waiter came up. He ordered a coffee for himself and a lemonade for Karl. Karl wondered if they ate children.

"I'm sure the reports are exaggerated," said the stranger. "A few isolated cases."

"Perhaps." Senor Glogauer put both his hands over the nob of his cane. "But I fear that if they come here I – or my son – might be one of those 'isolated cases'. We should be just as dead, I think."

The stranger laughed. "I take your point, senor." He turned in his chair and looked out at the life of the Parque. "But at least Cuba will be master of her own fate when this is over."

"Possibly." Senor Glogauer watched the waiter setting down his coffee.

"You have no sympathy with the insurgents?"

"None. Why should I? They have disrupted my business."

"Your view is understandable, senor. Well, I have work

to do." The stranger rose. Karl thought how ill and tired the man looked. He put on his own, slightly grubby, Panama. "It has been pleasant talking with you, senor. Good day."

"Good day, senor." Senor Glogauer pointed to the vacant chair and gratefully Karl went to it, sitting down. The lemonade was warm. It tasted of flies, thought Karl. He looked up at the huge electric fans rattling round and round on the ceiling. They had only been installed last year, but already there were specks of rust on their blades.

A little later, when they were leaving the Café Inglaterra, on their way across the Parque to where Senor Glogauer's carriage waited, a Spanish officer halted in front of them and saluted. He had four soldiers with him. They looked bored. "Senor Glogauer?" The Spaniard gave a slight bow and brought his heels together.

"Yes." Senor Glogauer frowned. "What is it, captain?"

"We would like you to accompany us, if you please."

"To where? For what?"

"A security matter. I do apologize. You are the father of Wilhelm Glogauer, are you not?"

"I have disowned my son," said Karl Glogauer's father grimly. "I do not support his opinions."

"You know what his opinions are?"

"Vaguely. I understand he is in favour of a break with Spain."

"I think he is rather more active a supporter of the insurgent cause than that, senor." The captain glanced at Karl as if sharing a joke with him. "Well, if you will now come with us to our headquarters, we can sort this whole thing out quickly."

"Must I come? Can't you ask me your questions here?"

"No. What about the boy?"

"He will come with his father." For a moment Karl thought that his father's decision was made from fear, that his father needed Karl's moral support. But that was silly, for his father was such a proud, self-reliant man.

With the soldiers behind them, they walked out of the Parque Central and up Obispo Street until they reached a gateway guarded by more soldiers. They went through the gate and into a courtyard. Here the captain dismissed the soldiers and gestured for Senor Glogauer to precede him into the building. Slowly, with dignity, Senor Glogauer ascended the steps and entered the foyer, one hand on his cane, the other grasping Karl's hand.

"And now this way, senor." The captain indicated a dark passage with many doors leading off it on both sides. They walked down this. "And down these steps, senor." Down a curving flight of steps into the basement of the building. The lower passage was lit by oil-lamps.

And another flight of steps.

"Down, please."

And now the smell was worse even than the smell of the Prado. Senor Glogauer took out a pure white linen handkerchief and fastidiously wiped his lips. "Where are we, senor captain?"

"The cells, Senor Glogauer. This is where we question prisoners and so on."

"You are not – I am not –?"

"Of course not. You are a private citizen. We only seek your help, I assure you. Your own loyalty is not in question."

Into one of the cells. There was a table in it. On the table was a flickering oil lamp. The lamp cast shadows which danced sluggishly. There was a strong smell of damp, of sweat, of urine. One of the shadows groaned. Senor Glogauer started and peered at it. "Mother of God!"

"I am afraid it is your son, senor. As you see. He was captured only about twenty miles from the city. He claimed that he was a small planter from the other side of the island. But we found his name in his wallet and someone had heard of you – your cigars, you know, which are so good. We put two and two together and then you – thank you very much – confirmed that your son was an insurgent. But we wanted to be sure this was your son, naturally, and not someone who had managed merely to get hold of his papers. And again, we thank you."

"Karl. Leave," said Senor Glogauer, remembering his other son. His voice was shaking. "At once."

51

"The sergeant at the door," said the officer, "perhaps he will give you a drink."

But Karl had already seen the dirty steel butcher's hooks on which Willi's wrists had been impaled, had seen the blue and yellow flesh around the wounds, the drying blood. He had seen Willi's poor, beaten face, his scarred body, his beast's eyes. Calmly, he came to a decision. He looked up the corridor. It was deserted.

When his father eventually came out of the cell, weeping and asking to be pardoned and justifying himself and calling upon God and cursing his son all at the same time, Karl had gone. He was walking steadily, walking on his little legs towards the outskirts of the city, on his way to find the insurgents still at liberty.

He intended to offer them his services.

— And why do you dislike Americans?
— I don't like the way some of them think they own the world.
— But didn't your people think that for centuries? Don't they still?
— It's different.
— And why do you collect model soldiers?
— I just do. It's relaxing. A hobby.
— Because you can't manipulate real people so easily?
— Think what you like. Karl turns over on the bed and immediately regrets it. But he lies there.

He feels the expected touch on his spine. Now you are feeling altogether more yourself, aren't you, Karl?

Karl's face is pressed into the pillow. He cannot speak.

The man's body presses down on his and for a moment he smiles. Is this what they mean by the White Man's Burden?

— Ssssssshhhhh, says the black man.

What Would You Do? (5)

You have three children.

One is eight years old. A girl.

One is six years old. A girl.

One is a few months old. A boy.

You are told that you can save any two of them from death, but not all three. You are given five minutes to choose.

Which one would you sacrifice?

6

London Sewing Circle: 1905: A Message

One would have thought that the meaning of the word "sweating" as applied to work was sufficiently obvious. But when "the Sweating System" was inquired into by the Committee of the House of Lords, the meaning became suddenly involved. As a matter of fact the sweater was originally a man who kept his people at work for long hours. A schoolboy who "sweats" for his examination studies for many hours beyond his usual working day. The schoolboy meaning of the word was originally the trade meaning.

But of late years the sweating system has come to mean an unhappy combination of long hours and low pay. "The sweater's den" is a workshop – often a dwelling room as well – in which, under the most unhealthy conditions, men and women toil for from sixteen to eighteen hours a day for a wage barely sufficient to keep body and soul together.

The sweating system, as far as London is concerned, exists chiefly at the East End, but it flourishes also in the West, notably in Soho, where the principal "sweating trade", tailoring, is now largely carried on. Let us visit the East End first, for here we can see the class which has largely contributed to the evil – the destitute foreign Jew – place his alien foot for the first time upon the free soil of England.

LIVING LONDON, *by George R. Sims*
Cassell & Co. Ltd., 1902.

Karl turns onto his side. He is aching. He is weeping.

– Did I promise you pleasure? asks the tall, black man as he wipes his hands on a hotel towel and then stretches and then yawns. – Did I?

– No. Karl's voice is muffled and small.

– You can leave whenever you wish.

– Like this?

– You'll get used to it. After all, millions of others have . . .

– Have you known them all?

The black man parts the curtain. It is now pitch dark outside and it is silent. – Now that's a leading question, he says. – The fact is, Karl, you are intrigued by all these new experiences. You welcome them. Why be a hypocrite?

– I'm not the hypocrite.

The black man grins and wags a chiding finger. Don't take it out on me, man. That wouldn't be very liberal, would it?

– I never was very liberal.

– You've been very liberal to me. The black man rolls his eyes in a comic grimace. Karl has seen the expression earlier. He begins to tremble again. He looks at his own brown hands and he tries to make his brain see all this in a proper, normal light.

He is eleven. A dark, filthy room. Many little sounds.

The black man says from beside the window: Come here, Karl.

Automatically Karl hauls himself from the bed and begins to make his way across the floor.

He remembers his mother and the tin of paint she threw at him which missed and ruined her wallpaper. You don't love me, he had said. Why should I? she had replied. He had been fourteen, perhaps, and ashamed of the question once he had asked it.

He is eleven. Many little regular sounds.

He approaches the black man. – That will do, Karl, says the black man.

Karl stops.

The black man approaches him. Under his breath he is humming "Old Folks At Home". Kneeling on the carpet,

Karl begins to sing the words in an exaggerated minstrel accent.

KARL WAS ELEVEN. His mother was thirty. His father was thirty five. They lived in London. They had come to London from Poland three years earlier. They had been escaping a pogrom. On their way, they had been robbed of most of their money by their countrymen. When they had arrived at the dockside, they had been met by a Jew who said he was from the same district as Karl's father and would help them. He had taken them to lodgings which had proved poor and expensive. When Karl's father ran out of money the man had loaned him a few shillings on his luggage and, when Karl's father could not pay him back, had kept the luggage and turned them out onto the street. Since then, Karl's father had found work. Now they all worked, Karl, his mother and his father. They worked for a tailor. Karl's father had been a printer in Poland, an educated man. But there was not enough work for Polish printers in London. One day Karl's father hoped that a job would become vacant on a Polish or Russian newspaper. Then they would become respectable again, as they had been in Poland.

At present, both Karl, his mother and his father all looked rather older than their respective ages. They sat together at one corner of the long table. Karl's mother worked a sewing machine. Karl's father sewed the lapel of a jacket. Around the table sat other groups – a man and a wife, three sisters, a mother and daughter, a father and son, two brothers. They all had the same appearance, were dressed in threadbare clothes of black and brown. The women's mouths were tight shut. The men mostly had thin, straggly beards. They were not all Polish. Some were from other countries: Russia, Bohemia, Germany and elsewhere. Some could not even speak Yiddish and were therefore incapable of conversing with anyone not from their own country.

The room in which they worked was lit by a single gas jet in the centre of the low ceiling. There was a small window, but it had been nailed up. The walls were of naked plaster through which could be seen patches of damp brick. Although it was winter, there was no fire in the room and the only heat came from the bodies of the workers. There was a fireplace in the room, but this was used to store the scraps of discarded material which could be re-used for padding. The smell of the people was very strong, but now few of them really noticed it, unless they left the room and came back in again, which was rarely. Some people would stay there for days at a time, sleeping in a corner and eating a bowl of soup someone would bring them, before starting work again.

A week ago, Karl had been there when they had discovered that the man whose coughing they had all complained about had not woken up for seven hours. Another man had knelt down and listened at the sleeping man's chest. He had nodded to the sleeping man's wife and sister-in-law and together they had carried him from the room. Neither the wife nor the sister-in-law came back for the rest of the day and it seemed to Karl that when they did return the wife's whole soul had not been in her work and her eyes were redder than usual, but the sister-in-law seemed much the same. The coughing man had not returned at all and, of course, Karl reasoned, it was because he was dead.

Karl's father laid down the coat. It was time to eat. He left the room and returned shortly with a small bundle wrapped in newspaper, a single large jug of hot tea. Karl's mother left her sewing machine and signed to Karl. The three of them sat in the corner of the room near the window while Karl's father unwrapped the newspaper and produced three cooked herrings. He handed one to each of them. They took turns to sip from the tea-jug. The meal lasted ten minutes and was eaten in silence. Then they went back to their place at the table, having carefully cleaned their fingers on the newspaper, for Mr. Armfelt would fine them if he discovered any grease spots on the clothes they were making.

Karl looked at his mother's thin, red fingers, at his father's lined face. They were no worse off than the rest.

That was the phrase his father always used when he and

his mother crawled into their end of the bed. Once he had prayed every night. Now that phrase was the nearest he came to a prayer.

The door opened and the room became a little more chill. The door closed. A short young man wearing a black bowler hat and a long overcoat stood there, blowing on his fingers. He spoke in Russian, his eyes wandering from face to face. Few looked up. Only Karl stared at him.

"Any lad like to do a job for me?" said the young man. "Urgent. Good money."

Several of the workers had his attention now, but Karl had already raised his hand. His father looked concerned, but said nothing.

"You'll do fine," said the young man. "Five shillings, And it won't take you long, probably. A message."

"A message where?" Like Karl, Karl's father spoke Russian as well as he spoke Polish.

"Just down to the docks. Not far. I'm busy, or I'd go myself. But I need someone who knows a bit of English, as well as Russian."

"I speak English," said Karl in English.

"Then you're definitely the lad I need. Is that all right?" glancing at Karl's father. "You've no objection?"

"I suppose not. Come back as soon as you can, Karl. And don't let anybody take your money from you." Karl's father began to sew again. His mother turned the handle of the sewing-machine a trifle faster, but that was all.

"Come on, then," said the young man.

Karl got up.

"It's pelting down out there," said the young man.

"Take the blanket, Karl," said his father.

Karl went to the corner and picked up the thin scrap of blanket. He draped it round his shoulders. The young man was already clumping down the stairs. Karl followed.

Outside in the alley it was almost as dark as night. Heavy rain swished down and filled the broken street with black pools in which it seemed you could fall and drown. A dog leaned in a doorway, shivering. At the far end of the alley were the lights of the pub. Blinds were drawn in half the windows of the buildings lining both sides of the street. In some of the remaining windows could be seen faint, ghostly lights. A voice was shouting, but whether it was in this alley or the next one, Karl couldn't tell. The shouting stopped. He huddled deeper into the blanket.

"You know Irongate Stairs?" The young man looked rapidly up and down the alley.

"Where the boats come ashore?" said Karl.

"That's right. Well, I want you to take this envelope to someone who's landing from the *Solchester* in an hour or so. Tell no one you have the envelope, save this man. And mention the man's name as little as you can. He may want your help. Do whatever he asks."

"And when will you pay me?"

"When you have done the work."

"How will I find you?"

"I'll come back here. Don't worry, I'm not like your damned masters! I won't go back on my word." The young man lifted his head almost proudly. "This day's work could see an end to what you people have to suffer."

He handed Karl the envelope. On it, in Russian, was written a single word, a name: KOVRIN.

"Kovrin," said Karl, rolling his r. "This is the man?"

"He's very tall and thin," said his new employer. "Probably wearing a Russian cap. You know the sort of thing people wear when they first come over. A very striking face, I'm told."

"You've not met him?"

"A relative, come to look for work," said the young man somewhat hastily. "That's enough. Go, before you're too late. And tell no one save him that you have met me, or there'll be no money for you. Get it?"

Karl nodded. The rain was already soaking through his blanket. He tucked the envelope into his shirt and began to trot along the alley, avoiding the worst of the puddles. As he passed the pub, a piano began to play and he heard a cracked voice singing:

Don't stop me 'arf a pint o' beer,
It's the only fing what's keepin' me alive.
I don't mind yer stoppin' of me corfee and me tea,
But 'arf a pint o' beer a day is medicine to me.
I don't want no bloomin' milk or eggs,
And to buy them I'll find it very dear.
If you want to see me 'appy and contented all me life,
Don't stop me 'arf a pint o' beer!

Now I'm a chap what's moderate in all I 'ave to drink,
And if that's wrong, then tell me what is right . . .

Karl did not hear all the words properly. Besides, such songs all sounded the same to him, with virtually the same tunes and the same sentiments. He found the English rather crude and stupid, particularly in their musical tastes. He wished he were somewhere else. Whenever he wasn't working, when he could daydream quite cheerfully as he sewed pads into jackets, this feeling overwhelmed him. He longed for the little town in Poland he could barely remember, for the sun and the cornfields, the snows and the pines. He had never been clear about why they had had to leave so hastily.

Water filled his ruined shoes and made the cloth of his trousers stick to his thin legs. He crossed another alley. There were two or three English boys there. They were scuffling about on the wet cobbles. He hoped they wouldn't see him. There was nothing that cheered bored English boys up so much as the prospect of baiting Karl Glogauer. And it was important that he shouldn't lose the letter, or fail to deliver it. Five shillings was worth nearly two days work. In an hour he would make as much as he would normally make in thirty-six. They hadn't seen him. He reached the broader streets and entered Commercial Street which was crowded with slow-moving traffic. Everything, even the cabs, seemed beaten down by the grey rain. The world was a place of blacks and dirty whites, spattered with the yellow of gas-lamps in the windows of the pie-and-mash shops, the second-hand clothes shops, the pubs and the pawnshops. Plodding drey horses threatened to smash their heads against the curved green fronts of the trams or the omnibuses; carters swore at their beasts, their rivals and themselves. Swathed in rubber, or canvas, or gaberdine, crouching beneath umbrellas, men and women stumbled into each other or stepped aside just in time. Through all these dodged Karl with his message in his shirt, crossing Aldgate and running down the dismal length of Leman Street, past more pubs, a few dismal shops, crumbling houses, brick walls which seemed to have no function but to block light from the street, a police station with a blue lamp gleaming over its door, another wall plastered with advertisements for meat-drinks, soaps, bicycles, nerve tonics, beers, money-lenders, political parties, newspapers, music-halls, jobs (No Irish or Aliens Need Apply), furniture on easy terms, the Army. The rain washed them down and made some of them look fresh again. Across Cable Street, down Dock Street, through another maze of alleys, even darker than the others, to Wapping Lane.

When he reached the River, Karl had to ask his way, for, in fact, he had lied when he had told the man he knew Irongate Stairs. People found his guttural accent hard to understand and lost patience with him quickly, but one old man gave him the direction. It was still some distance off. He broke into a trot again, the blanket drawn up over his head, so that he looked like some supernatural creature, a body without a skull, running mindlessly through the cold streets.

When he reached Irongate Stairs, the first boats were already bringing the immigrants ashore, for the ship itself could not tie up at the wharf. He saw that it was the right ship, a mass of red and black, belching oily smoke over the oily river, smoke which also seemed pressed down by the rain and which would not rise. The *Solchester* was a regular caller at Irongate Stairs, sailing twice a week from Hamburg with its cargo of Jews and political exiles. Karl had seen many identical people in his three years in Whitechapel. They were thin and there was hunger in their eyes; bewildered, bare-headed women, with shawls round their shoulders more threadbare than Karl's blanket, dragged their bundles from the boats to the wharf, trying at the same time to keep control of their scrawny children. A number of the men were quarrelling with the boatman, refusing to pay the sixpence which was his standard charge. They had been cheated so often on their journey that they were certain they were being cheated yet again. Others were staring in miserable astonishment at the blurred and blotted line of wharves and grim buildings which seemed to make up the entire city, hesitating before entering the dark archway which protected this particular wharf. The archway was crowded with loafers and touts all busily trying to confuse them, to seize their luggage, almost fighting to get possession of it.

Two policemen stood near the exit to Irongate Stairs, refusing to take part in any of the many arguments which broke out, unable to understand the many questions which the refugees put to them, simply smiling patronisingly and shaking their heads, pointing to the reasonably well-dressed man who moved anxiously amongst the people and asking questions in Yiddish or Lettish. Chiefly he wanted to know if the people had an address to go to. Karl recognised him. This was Mr. Somper, the Superintendent of the Poor Jews' Temporary Shelter. Mr. Somper had met them three years before. At that time Karl's father had been confident that he needed no such assistance. Karl saw that many of the newcomers were as confident as his father had been. Mr. Somper did his best to listen sympathetically to all the tales they told him – of robbery at the frontier, of the travel agent who told them they would easily find a good job in England, of the oppression they had suffered in their own countries. Many waved pieces of crumpled paper on which addresses were written in English – the names of friends or relatives who had already settled in London. Mr. Somper, his dark face clouded with care, saw to it that their baggage was loaded on to the waiting carts, assured those who tried to hang on to their bundles that they would not be stolen, united mothers with stray children and husbands with wives. Some of the people did not need his help and they looked as relieved as he did. These were going on to America and were merely transferring from one boat to another.

Karl could see no one of Kovrin's description. He was jostled back and forth as the Germans and the Roumanians and the Russians, many of them still wearing the embroidered smocks of their homeland, crowded around him, shrieking at each other, at the loafers and the officials, terrified by the oppressive skies and the gloomy darkness of the archway.

Another boat pulled in and a tall man stepped from it. He carried only a small bundle and was somewhat better dressed than those around him. He wore a long overcoat which was buttoned to the neck, a peaked Russian cap and there were high boots on his feet. Karl knew immediately that this was Kovrin. As the man moved through the crowd, making for the exit where the officials were checking the few papers the immigrants had, Karl ran up to him and tugged at his sleeve.

"Mr. Kovrin?"

The man looked surprised and hesitated before answering. He had pale blue eyes and high cheekbones. There was a redness on his cheekbones which contrasted rather strangely with his pale skin. He nodded. "Kovrin – yes."

"I have a letter for you, sir."

Karl drew the sodden envelope from his shirt. The ink had run, but Kovrin's name was still there in faint outline. Kovrin frowned and glanced about him before opening the envelope and reading the message inside. His lips moved slightly as he read. When he had finished, he looked down at Karl.

"Who sent you? Pesotsky?"

"A short man. He did not tell me his name."

"You know where he lives?"

"No."

"You know where this address is?" The Russian pointed at the letter.

"What is the address?"

Kovrin scowled at the letter and said slowly: "Trinity Street and Falmouth Road. A doctor's surgery. Southwark, is it?"

"That's on the other side of the river," said Karl. "A long walk. Or you could get a cab."

"A cab, yes. You speak English?"

63

"Yes, sir."

"You will tell the driver where we wish to go?"

There were fewer of the immigrants on Irongate Stairs now. Kovrin must have realised that he was beginning to look conspicuous. He seized Karl's shoulder and guided him up to the exit, showing a piece of paper to the official there. The man seemed satisfied. There was one cab standing outside. It was old and the horse and driver seemed even older. "There," murmured Kovrin in Russian, "that will do, eh?"

"It is a long way to Southwark, sir. I was not told . . ." Karl tried to break free of the man's grip. Kovrin hissed through his teeth and felt in the pocket of his greatcoat. He drew out half-a-sovereign and pushed it at Karl. "Will that do? Will that pay for your valuable time, you urchin?"

Karl accepted the money, trying to disguise the light of elation which had fired his eyes. This was twice what the young man had offered him – and he would get that as well if he helped the Russian, Kovrin.

He shouted up to the cabby. "Hey – this gentleman and I wish to go to Southwark. To Trinity Street. Get a move on, there!"

"Ye can pay, can ye?" said the old man, spitting. "I've 'ad trouble wi' you lot afore." He looked meaningfully around him at no-one. The rain fell on the sheds, on the patches of dirt, on the brick walls erected for no apparent purpose. Along the lane could just be seen the last of the immigrants, shuffling behind the carts which carried their baggage and their children. "I'll want 'arf in advance."

"How much?" Karl asked.

"Call it three bob – eighteenpence now – eighteenpence when we get there."

"That's too much."

"Take it or leave it."

"He wants three shillings for the fare," Karl told the Russian. "Half now. Have you got it?"

Wearily and disdainfully Kovrin displayed a handful of change. Karl took three sixpences and gave them to the driver.

"All right – 'op in," said the driver. He now spoke patronisingly, which was the nearest his tone could get to being actually friendly.

The hansom creaked and groaned as the cabby whipped his horse up. The springs in the seats squeaked and then the whole rickety contrivance was off, making quite rapid progress out of the dock area and heading for Tower Bridge, the nearest point of crossing into Southwark.

A boat was passing under the bridge, which was up. A line of traffic waited for it to be lowered again. While he waited Karl looked towards the West. The sky seemed lighter over that part of the city and the buildings seemed paler, purer, to him. He had only been to the West once and had seen the buildings of Parliament and Westminster Abbey in the sunshine. They were tall and spacious and he had imagined them to be the palaces of very great men. The cab jerked forward and began to move across the river, passing through a pall of smoke left behind by the funnel of the boat.

Doubtless the Russian, sitting in silence and glaring moodily out of the window, noticed no great difference between the streets on this side of the river, but Karl saw prosperity here. There were more food shops and there was more food sold in them. They went through a market where stalls sold shellfish, fried cod and potatoes, meat of almost every variety, as well as clothing, toys, vegetables, cutlery – everything one could possibly desire. With a fortune in his pocket, Karl's daydreams took a different turn as he thought of the luxuries they might buy; perhaps on Saturday after they had been to the Synagogue. Certainly, they could have new coats, get their shoes repaired, buy a piece of meat, a cabbage . . .

The cab pulled up on the corner of Trinity Street and Falmouth Road. The cabby rapped on the roof with his whip. "This is it."

They pushed open the door and descended. Karl took another three sixpences from the Russian and handed them up to the driver who bit them, nodded, and was off again, disappearing into Dover Street, joining the other traffic.

Karl looked at the building. There was a dirty brass plate on the wall by the door. He read: "Seamen's Clinic." He saw that the Russian was looking suspiciously at the plate, unable to understand the words. "Are you a sailor?" Karl asked. "Are you ill?"

"Be silent," said Kovrin. "Ring the bell. I'll wait here." He put his hand inside his coat. "Tell them that Kovrin is here."

Karl went up the cracked steps and pulled the iron bell handle. He heard a bell clang loudly. He had to wait some time before the door was opened by an old man with a long white forked beard and hooded eyes. "What do you want, boy?" said the man in English.

Karl said, also in English: "Kovrin is here." He jerked a thumb at the tall Russian standing in the rain behind him.

"Now?" The old man smiled in unsuppressed delight. "Here? Kovrin!"

Kovrin suddenly sprang up the steps, pushing Karl aside. After a perfunctory embrace, he and the old man went inside, speaking rapidly to each other in Russian. Karl followed them. He was hoping to earn another half guinea. He heard little of what they said, just a few words – "St. Petersburg" – "prison" – "commune" – "death" – and one very potent word he had heard many times before – "Siberia". Had Kovrin escaped from Siberia? There were quite a few Russians who had. Karl had heard some of them talking.

In the house, he could see that it was evidently no longer a doctor's surgery. The house, in fact, seemed virtually derelict, with hardly any furniture but piles of paper all over the place. Many bundles of the same newspaper stood in one corner of the hall. Over these a mattress had been thrown and was serving someone as a bed. Most of the newspapers were in Russian, others were in English and in what Karl guessed was German. There were also handbills which echoed the headlines of the newspapers: PEASANTS REVOLT, said one. CRUEL SUPPRESSION OF DEMOCRATIC RIGHTS IN ST. PETERSBURG, said another. Karl decided that these people must be political. His father had always told him to steer clear of "politicals", they were always in trouble with the police. Perhaps he should leave?

But then the old man turned to him and smiled kindly. "You look hungry. Will you eat with us?"

It would be foolish to turn down a free meal. Karl nodded. They entered a big room warmed by a central stove. From the way in which the room was laid out, Karl guessed that this had been the doctor's waiting room. But now it, too, stored bales of paper. He could smell soup. It made his mouth water. At the same time there came a peculiar sound from below his feet. Growling, thumping, clanking: it was as if some awful monster were chained in the cellar, trying to escape. The room shook. The old man led Karl and Kovrin into what had once been the main surgery. There were still glass instrument cases along the walls. Over in one corner they had installed a big, black cooking range and at this stood a woman, stirring an iron pot. The woman was quite pretty, but she looked scarcely less tired than Karl's mother. She ladled thick soup into an earthenware bowl. Karl's stomach rumbled. The woman smiled shyly at Kovrin whom she plainly did not know, but had been expecting. "Who is the boy?" she asked.

"Karl," said Karl. He bowed.

"Not Karl Marx, perhaps?" laughed the old man, nudging Karl on the shoulder. But Karl did not recognise the name. "Karl Glogauer," he said.

The old man explained to the woman: "He's Kovrin's guide. Pesotsky sent him. Pesotsky couldn't come himself because he's being watched. To meet Kovrin, would have been to betray him to our friends ... Give the boy some soup, Tanya." He took hold of Kovrin's arm. "Now, Andrey Vassilitch, tell me everything that happened in Petersburg. Your poor brother, I have already heard about."

The rumbling from below grew louder. It was like an earthquake. Karl ate the tasty soup, sitting hunched over his bowl at the far end of the long bench. The soup had meat in it and several kinds of vegetables. At the other end of the bench Kovrin and the old man talked quietly together, hardly aware of their own bowls. Because of the noise from the cellar, Karl caught little of what they said, but they seemed to be speaking much of killing and torture and exile. He wondered why nobody else seemed to notice the noise.

The woman called Tanya offered him more soup. He wanted to take more, but he was already feeling very strange. The rich food was hard to hold down. He felt that he might vomit at any moment. But he persisted in keeping it in his stomach. It would mean he would not need to eat tonight.

He summoned the courage to ask her what the noise was. "Are we over an underground railway?"

She smiled. "It is just the printing press." She indicated a pile of leaflets on the bench. "We tell the English people what it is like in our country – how we are ground under by the aristocrats and the middle-classes."

"They want to know?" Karl asked the question cynically. His own experience had given him the answer.

Again she smiled. "Not many. The other papers are for our countrymen. They give news of what is going on in Russia and in Poland and elsewhere. Some of the papers go back to those countries . . ."

The old man looked up, putting a finger to his lips. He shook his head at Tanya and winked at Karl. "What you don't hear won't harm you, young one."

"My father was a printer in Poland," Karl said. "Perhaps you have work for him. He speaks both Russian, Polish and Yiddish. He is an educated man.

"There's little money in our work," said Tanya. "Is your father for the cause?"

"I don't think so," said Karl. "Is that necessary?"

"Yes," said Kovrin suddenly. His red cheekbones burned a little more hotly. "You must stop asking questions, boy. Wait a while longer. I think I will need to see Pesotsky."

Karl didn't tell Kovrin that he didn't know where to find Pesotsky, because he might get another sum of money for taking Kovrin back to Whitechapel. Perhaps that would do. Also, if he could introduce his father to one of these people, they might decide to give him a job anyway. Then the family would be respectable again. He looked down at

68

his clothes and felt miserable. They had stopped steaming and were now almost dry.

An hour later the noise from below stopped. Karl hardly noticed, for he was almost asleep with his head on his arms on the table. Someone seemed to be reciting a list to what had been the rhythm of the printing press.

"Elizelina Kralchenskaya – prison. Vera Ivanovna – Siberia. Dmitry Konstantinovitch – dead. Yegor Semyonitch – dead. Dukmasovs – all three dead. The Lebezyatnikovna sisters – five years prison. Klinevich, dead. Kudeyarov, dead. Nikolayevich, dead. Pervoyedov, dead. Petrovich, dead. And I heard they found Tarasevich in London and killed him."

"That's so. A bomb. Every bomb they use on us confirms the police in their view. We're always blowing ourselves up with our bombs, aren't we?" The old man laughed. "They've been after this place for months. One day a bomb will go off and the newspapers will report the accident – another bunch of Nihilists destroy themselves. It is easier to think that. What about Cherpanski? I heard he was in Germany..."

"They rooted him out. He fled. I thought he was in England. His wife and children are said to be here."

"That's so."

Karl fell asleep. He dreamed of respectability. He and his father and mother were living in the Houses of Parliament. But for some reason they were still sewing coats for Mr. Armfelt.

Kovrin was shaking him. "Wake up, boy. You've got to take me to Pesotsky now."

"How much?" Karl said blearily.

Kovrin smiled bitterly. "You're learning a good lesson, aren't you?" He put another half-guinea on the table. Karl picked it up. "You people..." Kovrin began, but then he shrugged and turned to the old man. "Can we get a cab?"

"Not much chance. You'd best walk, anyway. It will be a degree safer."

Karl pulled his blanket round him and stood up. He was reluctant to leave the warmth of the room but at the same time he was anxious to show his parents the wealth he had earned for them. His legs were stiff as he walked from the room and went to stand by the front door while Kovrin exchanged a few last words with the old man.

Kovrin opened the door. The rain had stopped and the night was very still. It must be very late, thought Karl.

The door closed behind them. Karl shivered. He was not sure where they were, but he had a general idea of the direction of the river. Once there he could find a bridge and he would know where he was. He hoped Kovrin would not be too angry when he discovered that Karl could not lead him directly to Pesotsky. They began to walk through the cold, deserted streets, some of which were dimly lit by gaslamps. A few cats screeched, a few dogs barked and a few voices raised in anger came from the mean houses by which they passed. Once or twice a cab clattered into sight and they tried to hail it, but it was engaged or refused to stop for them.

Karl was surprised at how easily he found London Bridge. Once across the sullen blackness of the Thames he got his bearings and began to walk more confidently, Kovrin walking silently beside him.

In another half-an-hour they had reached Aldgate, brightened by the flaring lamps of the coffee-stall which stood open all night, catering to the drunkards reluctant to go home, to the homeless, to the shift workers and even to some gentlemen who had finished sampling the low-life of Stepney and Whitechapel and were waiting until they could find a cab. There were a few women there, too – haggard, sickly. In the glare of the stall, their garishly painted faces reminded Karl of the ikons he had seen in the rooms of the Russians who lived on the same floor as his family. Even their soiled silks and their faded velvets had some of the quality of the clothes the people wore in the ikons. Two of the women jeered at Karl and Kovrin as they passed through the pool of light and entered the gash of blackness which was the opening to the warren of alleys where Karl lived.

Karl was anxious to get home now. He knew he had been

away much longer than he had expected. He did not wish to give his parents concern.

He passed the dark and silent pub, Kovrin stepping cautiously behind him. He came to the door of the house. His parents might be sleeping now or they might still be working. They shared a room above the workroom.

Kovrin whispered: "Is this Pesotsky's. You can go now."

"This is where I live. Pesotsky said he would meet me here," Karl told him at last. He felt relieved now that this confession was off his chest. "He owes me five shillings, you see. He said he would come here and pay it. Perhaps he is waiting for us inside."

Kovrin cursed and shoved Karl into the unlit doorway. Karl winced in pain as the Russian's hand squeezed his shoulder high up, near the neck. "It will be all right," he said. "Pesotsky will come. It will be all right."

Kovrin's grip relaxed and he gave a huge sigh, putting his hand to his nose and rubbing it, hissing a tune through his teeth as he considered what Karl had told him. Karl pressed the latch of the door and they entered a narrow passage. The passage was absolutely dark.

"Have you a match?" Karl asked Kovrin.

Kovrin struck a match. Karl found the stump of candle and held it out for Kovrin to light. The Russian just managed to light the wick before the match burned his fingers. Karl saw that Kovrin had a gun in his other hand. It was a peculiar gun with an oblong metal box coming down in front of the trigger. Karl had never seen a picture of a gun like it. He wondered if Kovrin had made it himself.

"Now where?" Kovrin said. He displayed the gun in the light of the guttering candle. "If I think you've led me into a trap . . ."

"Pesotsky will come," said Karl. "It is not a trap. He said he would meet me here." Karl pointed up the uncarpeted stairway. "He may be there. Shall we see?"

Kovrin considered this and then shook his head. "You go. See if he is there and if he is bring him down to me. I'll wait."

Karl left the candle with Kovrin and began to grope his way up the two flights to the landing off which was the workroom. He had seen no lights at the window, but that was to be expected. Mr. Armfelt knew the law and protected himself against it. Few Factory Inspectors visited this part of Whitechapel, but there was no point in inviting their attention. If they closed his business, where else would the people find work? Karl saw a faint light under the door. He opened it. The gas-jet was turned, if anything, a trifle lower. At the table sat the women and the children and the men, bent over their sewing. Karl's father looked up as Karl came in. His eyes were red and bleary. He could hardly see and his hands shook. It was plain that he had been waiting up for Karl. Karl saw that his mother was lying in the corner. She was snoring.

"Karl!" His father stood up, swaying. "What happened to you?"

"It took longer than I expected, father. I have got a lot of money and there is more to come. And there is a man I met who might give you a job as a printer."

"A printer?" Karl's father rubbed his eyes and sat down on his chair again. It seemed he was finding it difficult to understand what Karl was saying. "Printer? Your mother was in despair. She wanted to ask the police to find you. She thought – an accident."

"I have eaten well, father, and I have earned a lot of money." Karl reached into his pocket. "This Russian gave it to me. He is very rich."

"Rich? You have eaten? Good. Well, you can tell me when we wake up. Go up now. I will follow with your mother."

Karl realised that his father was too tired to hear him properly. Karl had seen his father like this before.

"You go, father," he said. "I have slept, too. And I have some more business to do before I sleep again. That young man who came today. Has he returned?"

"The one who gave you the job?" His father screwed his eyes up and rubbed them. "Yes, he came back about four or five hours ago, asking if *you* had returned."

"He had come to pay me my money," said Karl. "Did he say he would be back?"

"I think he did. He seemed agitated. What is going on, Karl?"

"Nothing, father," Karl remembered the gun in Kovrin's hand. "Nothing which concerns us. When Pesotsky comes back it will all be finished. They will go away."

Karl's father knelt beside his mother, trying to wake her. But she would not wake up. Karl's father lay down beside his mother and was asleep. Karl smiled down at them. When they woke, they would be very pleased to see the twenty-five shillings he would, by that time, have earned. And yet something marred his feeling of contentment. He frowned, realising that it was the gun he had seen. He hoped Pesotsky would return soon and that he and Kovrin would go away for good. He could not send Kovrin off somewhere, because then Pesotsky would not pay him the five shillings. He had to wait.

He saw that a few of the others at the table were staring at him almost resentfully. Perhaps they were jealous of his good fortune. He stared back and they resumed their concentration on their work. He felt at that point what it must be like to be Mr. Armfelt. Mr. Amfelt was scarcely any richer than the people he employed, but he had power. Karl saw that power was almost as good as money. And a little money gave one a great deal of power. He stared in contempt around the room, at the mean-faced people, at his sprawled, snoring parents. He smiled.

Kovrin came into the room. The hand which had held the gun was now buried in his greatcoat pocket. His face seemed paler than ever, his red cheekbones even more pronounced. "Is Pesotsky here?"

"He is coming." Karl indicated his sleeping father. "My father said so."

"When?"

Karl became amused by Kovrin's anxiety. "Soon," he said.

The people at the table were all looking up again. One

young woman said: "We are trying to work here. Go some-where else to talk."

Karl laughed. The laughter was high-pitched and un-pleasant. Even he was shocked by it. "We will not be here much longer," he said. "Get on with your work, then."

The young woman grumbled but resumed her sewing.

Kovrin looked at them all in disgust. "You fools," he said, "you will always be like this unless you do something about it. You are all victims."

The young woman's father, who sat beside her, stitching the seam of a pair of trousers, raised his head and there was an unexpected gleam of irony in his eyes. "We are all vic-tims," he said, "comrade." His hands continued to sew as he stared directly at Kovrin. "We are all victims."

Kovrin glanced away. "That's what I said." He was dis-concerted. He stepped to the door. "I'll wait on the land-ing," he told Karl.

Karl joined him on the landing. High above, a little light filtered through a patched fanlight. Most of the glass had been replaced with slats of wood. From the room behind them the small sounds of sewing continued, like the noises made by rats as they searched the tenements for food.

Karl smiled at Kovrin and said familiarly: "He's mad, that old man. I think he meant you were a victim. But you are rich, aren't you, Mr. Kovrin?"

Kovrin ignored him.

Karl went and sat on the top stair. He hardly felt the cold at all. Tomorrow he would have a new coat.

He heard the street door open below. He looked up at Kovrin, who had also heard it. Karl nodded. It could only be Pesotsky. Kovrin pushed past Karl and swiftly descend-ed the stairs. Karl followed.

But when they reached the passage, the candle was still flickering and it was plain that no one was there. Kovrin frowned. His hand remained in the pocket of his coat. He peered into the back of the passage, behind the stairs. "Pes-otsky?"

There was no reply.

And then the door was flung open suddenly and Pesotsky

stood framed in it. He was hatless, panting, wild-eyed. "Christ! Is that Kovrin?" he gasped.

Kovrin said quietly. "Kovrin here."

"Now," said Karl. "My five shillings, Mr. Pesotsky."

The young man ignored the outstretched hand as he spoke rapidly to Kovrin. "All the plan's gone wrong. You shouldn't have come here . . ."

"I had to. Uncle Theodore said you knew where Cherpanski was hiding. Without Cherpanski, there is no point in —" Kovrin broke off as Pesotsky silenced him.

"They have been following me for days, our friends. They don't know about Cherpanski, but they do know about Theodore's damned press. It's that they want to destroy. But I'm their only link. That's why I've been staying away. I heard you'd been at the press and had left for Whitechapel. I was followed, but I think I shook them off. We'd better leave at once."

"My five shillings, sir," said Karl. "You promised."

Uncomprehending, Pesotsky stared at Karl for a long moment, then he said to Kovrin: "Cherpanski's in the country. He's staying with some English comrades. Yorkshire, I think. You can get the train. You'll be safe enough once you're out of London. It's the presses they're chiefly after. They don't care what we do here as long as none of our stuff gets back into Russia. Now, you'll want Kings Cross Station . . ."

The door opened again and two men stood there, one behind the other. Both were fat. Both wore black overcoats with astrakhan collars and had bowler hats on their heads. They looked like successful businessmen. The leader smiled.

"Here at last," he said in Russian. Karl saw that his companion carried a hat-box under his arm. It was incongruous; it was sinister. Karl began to retreat up the stairs.

"Stop him!" called the newcomer. From the shadows of the next landing stepped two men. They held revolvers. Karl stopped halfway up the stairs. Here was an explanation for the sound of the door opening which had brought them down.

"This is a good cover, Comrade Pesotsky," said the leader. "Is that your name, these days?"

Pesotsky shrugged. He looked completely dejected. Karl wondered who the well-dressed Russians could be. They acted like policemen, but the British police didn't employ foreigners, he knew that much.

Kovrin laughed. "It's little Captain Minsky, isn't it? Or have you changed your name, too?"

Minsky pursed his lips and came a few paces into the passage. It was obvious that he was puzzled by Kovrin's recognition. He peered hard at Kovrin's face.

"I don't know you."

"No," said Kovrin quietly. "Why have they transferred you to the foreign branch? Were your barbarities too terrible even for St. Petersburg?"

Minsky smiled, as if complimented. "There is so little work for me in Petersburg these days," he said. "That is always the snag for a policeman. If he is a success, he faces unemployment."

"Vampire!" hissed Pesotsky. "Aren't you satisfied yet? Must you drink the last drop of blood?"

"It is a feature of your kind, Pesotsky," said Minsky patiently, "that everything must be coloured in the most melodramatic terms. It is your basic weakness, if I might offer advice. You are failed poets, the lot of you. That is the worst sort of person to choose a career in politics."

Pesotsky said sulkily: "Well, *you've* failed this time, anyway. This isn't the printing press. It's a sweatshop."

"I complimented you once on your excellent cover," said Minsky. "Do you want another compliment?"

Pesotsky shrugged. "Good luck in your search, then."

"We haven't time for a thorough search," Minsky told him. He signed to the man with the hatbox. "We, too, have our difficulties. Problems of diplomacy and so on." He took a watch from within his coat. "But we have a good five minutes, I think."

Karl was almost enjoying himself. Captain Minsky really did believe that the printing press was hidden here.

"Shall we begin upstairs?" Minsky said. "I understand that's where you were originally."

"How could a press be upstairs," Pesotsky said. "These rotten boards wouldn't stand the weight."

"The last press was very neatly distributed through several rooms," Minsky told him. "Lead on, please."

They ascended the stairs to the first landing. Karl guessed that the occupants of these rooms were probably awake and listening behind their doors. He once again experienced a thrill of superiority to them. One of the men who had been on the landing shook his head and pointed up the next flight of stairs.

The seven of them went up slowly. Captain Minsky had his revolver in his gloved hand. His three men also carried their revolvers, trained on the wretched Pesotsky and the glowering Kovrin. Karl led the way. "This is where my father and mother work," he said. "It is not a printers."

"They are disgusting," said Minsky to his lieutenant with the hatbox. "They are so swift to employ children for their degraded work. There's a light behind that door. Open it up, boy."

Karl opened the door of the workroom, fighting to hide his grin. His mother and father were still asleep. The young woman who had complained before looked up and glared at him. Then all seven had pushed into the room.

Minsky said: "Oh, you do look innocent. But I know what you're really up to here. Where's the press?"

Now everyone put down their work and looked at him in astonishment as he kicked at the wall in which the fireplace was set. It rang hollow, but that was because it was so thin. There was an identical room on the other side. But it satisfied Minsky. "Put that in here," he told the man with the hatbox. "We must be leaving."

"Have you found the press, then?" Karl grinned openly.

Minsky struck him across the mouth with the barrel of his revolver. Karl moaned as blood filled his right cheek. He fell back over the sleeping bodies of his parents. They stirred.

Kovrin had drawn his gun. He waved it to cover all four

77

members of the Secret Police. "Drop your weapons," he shouted. "You – pick that hatbox up again."

The man glanced uncertainly at Minsky. "It's already triggered. We have a few moments."

Karl realised there was a bomb in the box. He tried to wake his father to tell him. Now the people who had been working were standing up. There was a noisy outcry. Children were weeping, women shrieking, men shouting.

Kovrin shot Minsky.

One of Minsky's men shot Kovrin. Kovrin fell back through the door and Karl heard him fall to the landing outside. Pesotsky flung himself at the man who had shot Kovrin. Another gun went off and Pesotsky fell to the floor, his fists clenched, his stomach pulsing out blood.

Karl's father woke up. His eyes widened at what they saw. He clutched Karl to him. Karl's mother woke up. She whimpered. Karl saw that Minsky was dead. The other three men hurried from the room and began to run downstairs.

An explosion filled the room.

Karl was protected by his parents' bodies, but he felt them shudder and move as the explosion hit them. He saw a little boy strike the far wall. He saw the window shatter. He saw the door collapse, driven out into the darkness of the stairwell. He saw fire send tendrils in all directions and then withdraw them. The workbench had come to rest against the opposite wall. It was black and broken. The wall was naked brick and the brick was also black. Something was roaring. His vision was wiped out and he saw only whiteness.

He closed his eyes and opened them again. His eyes stung but he could see dimly, even though the gas jet had been blown out. Throughout the room there was a terrible silence for a second or two. Then they began to groan.

Soon the room was filled with their groaning. Karl saw that the floor sloped where it had not sloped before. He saw that part of the outer wall had split. Through this great crack came moonlight. Black things shifted about on the floor.

Now the entire street outside was alive with noise. Voices came from below and from above. He heard feet on the stairs. Someone shone a lamp onto the scene and then retreated with a gasp. Karl stood up. He was unhurt, although his skin was stinging and he had some bruises. He saw that his father had no right hand any more and that blood was oozing from the stump. He put his head to his father's chest. He was still breathing. His mother held her face. She told Karl that she was blind.

Karl went out onto the landing and saw the crowd on both the upper and the lower stairs. The man with the lamp was Mr. Armfelt. He was in his nightshirt. He looked unwell and was staring at the figure who leaned on the wall on the opposite side of the door. It was Kovrin. He was soaked in blood, but he was breathing and the strange gun was still in his right hand. Karl hated Kovrin, whom he saw as the chief agent of this disaster. He went and looked up into the tall Russian's eyes. He took the pistol from Kovrin's limp hand. As if the pistol had been supporting him, Kovrin crashed to the floor as soon as it was removed from his grasp. Karl looked down at him. Kovrin was dead. None of the watchers spoke. They all looked on as if they were the audience at some particularly terrifying melodrama.

Karl took the lamp from Mr. Armfelt and returned to the room.

Many of the occupants were dead. Karl saw that the young woman was dead, her body all broken and tangled up with that of her father, the man who had said "We are all victims". Karl sniffed. Minsky's body had been blown under the shattered bench, but Pesotsky had been quite close to the recess where Karl and his parents had lain. Although wounded, he was alive. He was chuckling. With every spasm, more blood gushed from his mouth. He said thickly to Karl: "Thanks – thanks." He waited for the blood to subside. "They've blown up the wrong place, thanks to you. What luck!"

Karl studied the gun he had taken from Kovrin. He assumed that it was basically the same as a revolver and contained at least another five bullets. He held it in both hands and, with both his index fingers on the trigger, squeezed. The gun went off with a bang and a flash and Karl's knuckles were driven back into his face, cutting his lip again. He lowered the gun and picked up the lamp which he had placed on the floor. He advanced on Pesotsky and held the lamp over the body. The bullet had driven through one of Pesotsky's eyes and Pesotsky was dead. Karl searched through Pesotsky's bloodsoaked clothes and found two shillings and some coppers. He counted it. Three shillings and eightpence in all. Pesotsky had lied to him. Pesotsky had not possessed five shillings. He spat on Pesotsky's face.

At the sound of the shot, the people on the stairs had withdrawn a few paces. Only Mr. Armfelt remained where he was. He was talking rapidly to himself in a language Karl did not recognise. Karl tucked the gun into the waistband of his trousers and turned Kovrin's corpse over. In the pockets of the greatcoat he found about ten pounds in gold. In an inner pocket he found some documents, which he discarded, and about fifty pounds in paper money. Carrying the lamp high he shone it on the blind face of his mother and on the pain-racked face of his father. His father was awake and saying something about a doctor.

Karl nodded. It was sensible that they should get a doctor as soon as possible. They could afford one now. He held out the money so that his father could see it all, the white banknotes and the bright gold. "I can look after you both, father. You will get better. It doesn't matter if you cannot work. We shall be respectable."

He saw that his father could still not quite understand. With a shake of his head, Karl crouched down and put a kindly hand on his father's shoulder. He spoke clearly and gently, as one might address a very young child who had failed to gather it was about to receive a birthday present and was not showing proper enthusiasm.

"We can go to *America*, father."

He inspected the wrist from which most of the hand had been blown. With some of the rags, he bandaged it, stopping the worst of the bleeding.

And then the sobs began to come up from his stomach.

80

He did not know why he was crying, but he could not control himself. The sobs made him helpless. His body was shaken by them and the noise he made was not very loud but it was the worst noise any of the listeners had heard that night. Even Mr. Armfelt, absorbed in his hysterical calculations, was dimly aware of the noise and he became, if anything, even more depressed.

– What do you think it can be? Something you ate? Do you want some aspirin?
– Aspirin won't do anything for me. I don't know what causes a migraine. A combination of things, maybe.
– Or merely a useful evasion, Karl. Like some forms of gout or consumption. One of those subtle diseases whose symptoms can only be transmitted by word of mouth.
– Thanks for your sympathy. Can I sleep now.
– What a time to get a headache. And you were just beginning to enjoy yourself, too.

What Would You Do? (6)

You live in a city.

A disaster has resulted in the collapse of society as you know it.

Public amenities, such as gas, electricity, telephones and postal services no longer exist. There is no piped water. Rats and other vermin proliferate in the piles of garbage which, uncollected, contaminate the city. Disease is rife. You have heard that things are equally bad in the country. There, strangers are attacked and killed if they try to settle. In some ways it is more dangerous in the country than it is in the city where gangs of predatory men and women roam the streets.

You are used to city life. You have a house, a car and you have obtained several guns from a gunshop you broke into. You raid shops and garages for fuel and food. You have a water purifier and a camp stove. You have a wife and three young children.

Do you think it would be better to go out into the country and take your chances in the wild, or would you try to work out a way of living and protecting yourself and your family in a city with which you are familiar?

7

Calcutta Flies: 1911: Doing Business

Ten years ago, an observer going to India with a fresh mind for its problems saw two great engines at work. One was the British Government, ruling the country according to its own canons of what would be best for the people. Its system of education in Western science and thought was shaking the old beliefs and social traditions. By securing justice and enforcing peace, it had set men's minds free to speculate and criticise. For India's future it had no definite plan; its ambitions, to all outward seeming, were confined to a steady growth of administrative efficiency. The other engine was the awakening of a national consciousness. It was feeding on the Western ideas provided by the British Government and the noble army of Christian missionaries, adapting them to its own purposes, and building on them a rising demand that the people should be given a larger share in their own destiny. Our observer could not help being impressed by how far the two engines were from working in parallel. There was friction and a general feeling of unsettlement. In 1908 a cautious measure of political advance had been offered when Lord Minto was Viceroy and Lord Morley was his "opposite number" in Whitehall. It was tainted, however, with an air of unreality which disquieted the officials and irritated the Indian politician. The cry grew loud for more rapid progress, "colonial self-government" was the slogan, and the professional classes (chiefly the lawyers) with an English education were busy in a wide-spread movement for a change in the methods of government. As in all nationalist movements, there was an extreme wing, which leaned to direct action, rather than the slower constitutional modes of agitation. In Eastern hyperbole they wrote and harangued about British tyranny and the duty of patriots to rise and become martyrs for freedom. What they thus conceived in poetic frenzy was translated into sinister prose by others. Anarchists are never lacking in any crowded population, especially when hunger is the bedfellow of so many. In India the section of violence had got into touch with revolutionary camps in Europe and the United States, and sporadic outbursts from 1907 onwards, including attempts on the life of two Viceroys and a Lieutenant-Governor, indicated the existence of subterranean conspiracy. Public opinion condemned it, but did little to check vehemence of language which continued to inflame weak minds. The whole position was one of anxiety. Would it ever be possible to reconcile the two forces which were rapidly moving towards conflict?

THE DOMINIONS AND DEPENDENCIES OF THE EMPIRE
*India by the Rt. Hon. Lord Meston, KCSI, LLD.
Collins, 1924.*

–*There! That's more like it, Karl! Ah! Better! Better! Now you're moving!*

Karl bucks and bounces, gasps and groans. His muscles ache, but he forces his body to make dramatic responses to every tiny stimulus. The black man cheers him on, yelling with delight.

– *Ah!* sings Karl. *Oh!*
Ah! Oh!

Up and down and from side to side, whinnying like a proud stallion, he carries the black man round the hotel

room on his back. His back is wet, but not from sperm or
sweat, for, in spite of all his shouts of pleasure, the black
man has not had an orgasm as far as Karl can tell. His
back is wet with just a drop or two of blood.

– Now you're moving! Now you're moving! shouts the
black man again. – Hurrah!

Karl is twelve. An orphan. Half-German, half-Indian. In
Calcutta. In 1911.

– Faster! Faster! The black man has produced a riding
crop and with it he flicks Karl's bouncing buttocks.
– Faster!

When Karl was fifteen, he left home to become a great
painter. He returned home three months later. He had been
turned down by the Art School. His mother had been very
sympathetic. She could afford to be.

– Faster! That's it! You're learning, Karl!

Karl is twelve. The red sun rises over red ships. Cal-
cutta . . .

The riding crop cracks harder and Karl gallops on.

KARL WAS TWELVE. His mother was dead. His father was
dead. His two sisters were sixteen and seventeen and he
did not often see them. He embarrassed them. Karl was in
business for himself and, all things considered, he was doing
pretty well.

He worked the docks along the Hooghly. He described
himself as an Agent. If something was wanted by the sailors or the passengers off the ships, he would either get it
for them or take them somewhere where they might obtain
it. He did better than the other boys in the same trade, for
he was quite light-skinned and he wore a European suit. He
spoke English and German perfectly and was fairly fluent
in most other languages, including a fair number of Indian
dialects. Because he knew when to be honest and who to
bribe, he was popular both with customers and suppliers
and people coming from the big red steamers would ask
after him when they landed, having been recommended to
him by friends. Because he was well-mannered and discreet, he was tolerated by most of the Indian and British

policemen on the docks (and he had done several of them good turns in his time, for he knew the importance of keeping in with the authorities). Karl was rumoured to be a millionaire (in rupees), but, because of his overheads, he was, in fact, worth only about a thousand rupees, which he banked with his friend in Barrackpore, some fifteen miles away, because it was safer. He was content with his relatively small profit and had worked out that by the time he was twenty he would be quite rich enough to set himself up in a respectable business of some kind in Central Calcutta.

Karl's only concession to his Indian mother was his turban. His turban was virtually his trademark and he was recognised by it throughout Calcutta. It was a black turban, of gleaming silk. Its single decoration was a small pin –an enamelled pin he had been given by a rather eccentric English lady who had sought his services a year or two back. The pin was white, gold and red and showed a crown with a scroll over it. On the scroll was written *Edward VII*. It had been made, the lady had told Karl, to commemorate the Coronation. The pin was therefore quite old and might be valuable. Karl felt it a fitting decoration for his black, silk turban.

Earlier that morning, Karl had been contacted by a young sailor who had offered to buy all the hemp Karl could procure by that afternoon. He had offered a reasonable price – though not an especially good one – and Karl had agreed. He knew that the young sailor had a customer in one of the European ports and that once his hemp arrived in Europe it would be several times more valuable than it was in Calcutta. But Karl was not worried. He would make his profit and it would be satisfactory. Everyone would be happy. The young sailor was English, but he was working on a French boat, the *Juliette*, currently taking on grain and indigo down at Kalna. The young sailor, whose name was Marsden, had come up on one of the river steamers.

Through the confusion of the dock strode Karl, walking as quickly as was sensible in the midday heat, dodging bicycles and donkeys and carts and men who were scarcely visible for the huge bundles on their backs. Karl was proud of his city, enjoying the profusion of different racial types, the many contrasts and paradoxes of Calcutta. When he was cursed, as he often was, he would curse back in the same language. When he was greeted by acquaintances he would give a little bow and salute them with cheeky condescension, aping the manner of the Lieutenant-Governor on one of his ceremonial processions through the city.

Karl swaggered a little as he crossed Kidderpore Bridge and walked across the Maidan. He imagined that London must look very much like this and had heard the Maidan compared to Hyde Park, although the Maidan was much bigger. The trees were mainly of the English variety and reminded Karl of the pictures he had seen of the English countryside. He passed close to the Cathedral, with its Gothic spire emerging from a mass of greenery and a large sheet of water in the foreground. One of his customers, whom he had taken on a tour of the city the year before, had said it recalled exactly the view over Bayswater from the bridge spanning the Serpentine. One day Karl would visit London and see for himself.

He swaggered a little as he crossed the Maidan. He always felt more relaxed and at home in the better part of town. Near Government House, he hailed a rickshaw with a lordly wave and told the boy to take him to the junction of Armenian Street and Bhudab Road. It was really not much further to walk, but he felt in an expansive mood. He leaned back in his seat and breathed the spiced air of the city. He had told Marsden, the sailor, that he could get him a hundred poundsworth of hemp if he wanted it. Marsden had agreed to bring a hundred pounds to Dalhousie Square that afternoon. It would be one of the largest single business deals Karl had pulled off. He hoped that his friend in Armenian Street would be able to supply him with all the hemp he needed.

His friend worked for one of the big shipping firms in Armenian Street. This friend was a messenger and made a number of trips in and out of Calcutta during the week. Almost every one of these trips yielded a certain supply of hemp which Karl's friend then stored in a safe place until contacted by Karl.

The rickshaw stopped at the corner of Bhubab Road and Karl descended to the pavement, giving the rickshaw boy – a man of about fifty – a generous tip.

The bustle in this part of town was of a different quality to that nearer the docks. It was more assured, more muted. People didn't push so much, or bellow at one, or shout obscene insults. And here, too, there were fewer people sharing considerably more money. Karl was considering Armenian Street as the site for his business when he opened it. It would probably be an Import/Export business of some kind. He began to walk, sighing with pleasure at the thought of his future. The bright sunshine and the blue sky served as a perfect background to the solid, imposing Victorian buildings, making them all the more imposing. Karl strolled in their shade, reading off their dignified signs as he passed. The signs were beautifully painted in black script, or Gothic gold or tasteful silver. There was nothing vulgar here.

Karl entered the offices of a well-known Shipping Company and asked for his friend.

When he had completed his business in Armenian Street, Karl took out his steel railway watch and saw he had plenty of time to lunch before meeting the young sailor. Dalhousie Square was only a short distance away. Karl had, in fact, decided on one of his regular meeting places in St. Andrew's Church – the Red Church as the Indians called it – which would be deserted that afternoon. He had chosen a spot not too far from Armenian Street because it was unwise to carry a full case of hemp around for too long. There was always the risk of an officious policeman deciding to find out what was in his case. On the other hand, St. Andrew's was almost next door to the Police Headquarters and therefore one of the least likely places, so Karl hoped the police would reason, to choose for an illegal transaction.

Karl lunched at the small hotel called The Imperial Indian Hotel in Cotton Street. It was run by a Bengali friend of his and served the most delicious curries in Calcutta. Karl had brought many a customer here and his enthusiastic recommendations were always genuine. The customers, too, were well-pleased. In return for this service, Karl could eat at The Imperial Indian Hotel whenever he wished.

He finished his lunch and passed the time of day with the manager of the restaurant before leaving. It was nearly three o'clock. Karl had arranged to meet Marsden at seven minutes past three. Karl always arranged to meet people at odd minutes past the hour. It was one of his superstitions.

The curry had settled well on his stomach and he moved unhurriedly through the city of his birth. His suit was as clean and as well-pressed as ever. His shirt was white and crisp and his black silk turban gleamed on his head like a fat, sleek cat. In fact Karl himself was almost purring. In a short time he would have a hundred pounds in his pocket. Fifty of that, of course, would go immediately to his friend in Armenian Street. Then there were a few other expenses, such as the one he had just incurred during his chat with the manager of the hotel restaurant, but there would at the end of the day be about forty pounds to bank with his friend in Barrackpore. A worthwhile sum. His own business was not too far away now.

Dalhousie Square was one of Karl's favourite spots in the city. He would often come here simply for pleasure but when he could he mixed business with pleasure and became an unofficial tourist guide. As this was one of the oldest parts of Calcutta, he could show people everything they expected. The original Fort William had once stood here and part of it was now the Customs House. Karl particularly enjoyed pointing out to the European ladies where the guard room of the Fort had been. This guard room had, in 1756, become the infamous Black Hole. Karl could describe the sufferings of the people more than adequately. He had had the satisfaction, more than once, of seeing sensitive English ladies faint away during his descriptions.

St. Andrew's Scottish Presbyterian Church stood in its own wooded grounds in which there were two large artificial ponds (in common with the Anglo-Indians, Karl called them "tanks") and the one drawback of the place was that it was infested with mosquitoes virtually all the year round. As Karl walked up the paved path between the trees, he saw a great cloud of flies swarming in the bars of light between the Grecian columns of the portico. The clock on the "Lal Girja's" tower stood at six minutes past three.

Karl opened the iron gate in the fence and went up the steps, swatting at mosquitoes as he did so. He killed them in a rather chiding, friendly way.

He entered the relatively cool and almost deserted church. There was no service today and the only other occupant, standing awkwardly in the aisle between the pews of plain, polished wood, was the young sailor, Marsden. His face was red and sticky with sweat. He was wearing a pair of cream-coloured shorts, and a somewhat dirty white shirt. His legs and his arms were bare and the mosquitoes were delighted.

Marsden plainly had not wanted to make a noise in the church for fear of attracting someone's attention, so he had not slapped at the mosquitoes which covered his face, arms, hands and legs. Instead he was vainly trying to brush them off him. They would fly up in a cloud and settle immediately, continuing their feast.

Marsden plainly had not wanted to make a noise in the "Good afternoon, Mr. Marsden, sir," said Karl, displaying the carpet bag containing the drug. "One hundred poundsworth, as promised. Have you the money?"

"I'm glad to see you," said Marsden. "I'm being eaten alive in here. What a place to choose! Is it always like this?"

"Usually, I'm afraid to say." Karl tried to sound completely English, but to his annoyance, he could still detect a slight lilt in his voice. The lilt, he knew, betrayed him.

The sailor held out his hand for the bag. Karl saw that red lumps were rising on virtually every spot of the man's bare skin. "Come on, then, old son," said Marsden, "let's see if it's the genuine article."

Karl smiled ingratiatingly. "It is one hundred percent perfect stuff, Mr. Marsden." He put the bag at his feet and spread his hands. "Can I say the same about your cash, sir?"

"Naturally you can. Of course you can. Don't say you don't trust me, you little baboo! It's me should be worrying."

"Then let me see the money, sir," Karl said reasonably. "I am sure you are an honourable man, but . . ."

"You're damned right I am! I won't have a bloody darkie . . ." Marsden looked round nervously, realising he had raised his voice and it was echoing through the church. He whispered: "I'm not have a bloody darkie telling me I'm a welsher. The money's back at the ship. I'd have been a fool to come here alone with a hundred quid on me, wouldn't I?"

Karl sighed. "So you do not have the money on your person, Mr. Marsden?"

"No I don't!"

"Then I must keep the bag until you bring the money," Karl told him. "I am sorry. Business is business. You agreed."

"I know what we agreed," said Marsden defensively. "But I've got to be certain. Show me the stuff."

Karl shrugged and opened the bag. The aroma of hemp was unmistakable.

Marsden leaned forward and sniffed. He nodded.

"How much money do you have with you?" said Karl. He was beginning to see that Marsden had been exaggerating when he had said he would buy as much as Karl could find.

Marsden shrugged. He put his hands in his pockets. "I don't know. It's mainly in rupees. About four pounds ten."

Karl sniggered. "It is not a hundred pounds."

"I can get it. Back at the ship."

"The ship is nearly fifty miles away, Mr. Marsden."

"I'll give it you tomorrow."

When Marsden jumped forward and grabbed up the bag, Karl didn't move. When Marsden pushed him aside

91

and ran with the bag up the aisle, Karl sat down in one of the pews. If Marsden really did have four pounds ten, then at least Karl would have lost nothing on the deal. He would return the bag to his friend in Armenian Street and wait until he had a proper customer.

A short while later the young Sikh from Delhi came into the church. He was holding the bag. The Sikh had been staying at the Imperial Indian Hotel and had had trouble paying his bill. The manager of the restaurant had told Karl this and Karl had told the Sikh how he could earn the money to pay for his room. The Sikh evidently did not relish working for Karl, but he had no choice. He handed Karl the bag.

"Did he have enough money?" Karl asked.

The Sikh nodded. "Is that all?"

"Excellent," Karl told him. "Where is Marsden now?"

"In the tank. He was probably drunk and fell in there. It happens to sailors, I hear, in Calcutta. He may drown. He may not."

"Thank you," said Karl.

He waited for the Sikh to leave and remained in the church for some minutes, watching the mosquitoes dancing in the light from the windows. He was a little disappointed, he had to admit. But sooner or later another deal would come, even if he had to work a trifle harder, and there was no doubt that his savings would increase, that his ambitions would be realised.

A priest appeared from behind the altar. He saw Karl and smiled at him. "You're early, laddie, if you've come for the choir practice."

– *You're learning, says the black man lasciviously. You see, I said you would.*

Karl smiles up at him and stretches. – *Yes, you said I would. It's funny . . .*

– *You were saying about that girl-friend of yours. The black man changes the subject.* – *How she became pregnant?*

– *That's right. Before the abortion reforms. It cost me the best part of two hundred pounds. Karl smiles.* – *A lot of uniforms.*

92

– But the other two were cheaper? The two before?

– They got those done themselves. I was always unlucky. I couldn't use those rubber things, that was the trouble. I'd just lose interest if I tried to put one on.

– None of your children were born?

– If you put it like that, no.

Let the next one be born. The black man puts his hand on the muscles of Karl's upper forearm.

Karl is astonished at this apparent expression of human feeling. – You're against abortion, then?

The black one rolls over and reaches for his cigarettes on the bedside table. They are Nat Sherman's Queen Size Cigaretellos, an obscure American brand which Karl hasn't seen before. Earlier he has studied the packet with some interest. He accepts one of the slim, brown cigarettes and lights up from the tip of the black man's. He enjoys the taste.

– You're against abortion, then? Karl repeats.

– I'm against the destruction of possibilities. Everything should be allowed to proliferate. The interest lies in seeing which becomes dominant. Which wins.

– Ah, says Karl, I see. You want as many pieces on the board as you can get.

– Why not?

What Would You Do? (7)

You are a refugee fleeing from a government which will kill you and your family if they catch you.

You reach the railway station and in a great deal of confusion manage to get your wife and children onto the train, telling them to find a seat while you get the luggage on board.

After a while you manage to haul your luggage into the train as it is leaving the station. You settle it in the corridor and go to look for your family.

You search both ends of the train and they are not there. Someone tells you that only half the train left, that the other half is going to another destination.

Could they have got into the other half by mistake?

What will you do?

Pull the communication cord and set off back to the station, leaving your luggage on the train?

Wait until you reach the next station, leave your luggage there and catch the next train back?

Hope that your family will remain calm and follow you to your ultimate destination on the next available train?

8

Quiet Days in Thann: 1918: Mixed Meat

Never, probably in the history of the world, not even in the last years of the Napoleonic domination, has there taken place such a display of warlike passion as manifested itself in the most civilised countries of Europe at the beginning of August, 1914. Then was seen how frail were the commercial and political forces on which modern cosmopolitanism had fondly relied for the obliteration of national barriers. The elaborate system of European finance which, in the opinion of some, had rendered war impossible no more availed to avert the catastrophe than the Utopian aspirations of international Socialism, or the links with which a common culture had bound together the more educated classes of the Continent. The world of credit set to work to adapt itself to conditions which seemed, for a moment, to threaten it with annihilation. The voices of the advocates of a world-wide fraternity and equality were drowned in a roar of hostile preparation. The great gulfs that separate Slav, Latin, Teuton, and Anglo-Saxon were revealed; and the forces which decide the destinies of the world were gauntly expressed in terms of racial antagonism.

HISTORY OF THE WAR *Part One*.
Published by "The Times", 1915.

– It's your turn now, says the black man. – If you like . . .

– I'm tired, says Karl.

– Oh, come now! Tired! Psychological tiredness, that's all! The black man pats him on the back. He gives Karl an encouraging grin, offering him the riding crop.

– No, says Karl. – Please, no . . .

– Well, I offered.

Karl is thirteen. His mother is twenty-nine. His father is dead, killed at Verdun in 1916. His mother has gone to live with her sister in a village near Thann, in Alsace . . .

– Leave me alone, says Karl.

– Of course. I don't want to influence you.

When Karl was thirteen he met a man who claimed to be his father. It was in a public lavatory somewhere in West London. "I'm your dad," the man had said. His stiff penis had been exposed. "Are you still at school, lad?" Karl had mumbled something and run out of the lavatory. He regretted his decision later because the man could have been his father, after all.

– Leave me in peace.

– You're a very moody chap, young Karl, laughs the black man.

He brings the riding crop down with a crack on Karl's back. Karl yells. He scrambles out of the bed and begins to get dressed – That's it, he says.

– I'm sorry, says the black man.   Please forgive me.

Karl is thirteen. He is now the provider for his mother and his aunt. The war continues not too far away. While it continues, Karl will survive . . .

– I misinterpreted you, that's all, says the black man. Please stay just a short while longer, eh?

– Why should I?

But Karl is weakening again.

KARL WAS THIRTEEN. His mother was twenty-nine. His father was dead, killed in the War. His mother's sister was twenty-six, also a widow. Where they lived there were many reminders of the war. It had been fought around here for a

96

while. Broken fences, smashed trees, craters filled with water, old trenches and ruins. Ploughmen did not like to plough the ground, for they always found at least one corpse.

Karl had found a gun. It was a good French rifle. He had found plenty of ammunition in the belt of the soldier. He had tried to get the soldier's boots, but the flesh inside them had swollen up too much. Besides, Karl was perfectly satisfied with the gun. With it, he was now able to earn a decent living. Few people in the villages around Thann could do that at present.

In a thick corduroy jacket and tweed knickerbockers secured below the knee with an English soldier's puttees, with a large German knapsack over his shoulder and the French rifle in the crook of his arm, Karl sat comfortably on a slab of masonry and smoked a cigarette, waiting.

It was close to sunrise and he had arrived at the ruined farmhouse about an hour earlier. Dawn was a yellow line on the horizon. He unpacked his German fieldglasses and began to scan the surrounding ground – mud, treestumps, ditches, trenches, craters, ruins ... all were shadowy, all still. Karl was looking for movement.

He saw a dog. It was quite big, but thin. It sauntered along the edge of a ditch, wagging its feathery tail. Karl put down his fieldglasses and picked up his rifle. He adjusted the sliding rearsight, tucked the stock firmly into his shoulder, braced his feet on the mound of brick, took precise aim and squeezed the trigger of the rifle. The stock banged into his shoulder and the gun jumped. There was a report and smoke. Karl lowered the rifle and took out his fieldglasses. The dog was not quite dead. He stood up, a thumb hooked into the strap of the knapsack. By the time he reached it, the dog would be dead.

As he skinned the animal, Karl kept his eyes peeled for other quarry. It was thin on the ground, these days. But, if anyone could get it, Karl could. He sawed off the head with the bayonet he carried for the purpose. The butcher in Thann did not ask questions when he bought Karl's loads of "mixed meat", but he did not like to be reminded too closely of the type of animal he was buying.

A little later Karl shot two rats and the cat which had been hunting them. He was amused by this exploit.

He wished he could have told someone of it. But his mother and aunt were squeamish. They preferred to believe he was hunting pigeons. Sometimes he did shoot a pigeon. He would take that home and give it to his mother to cook. "Part of the bag," he would say. It was just as well to keep up appearances.

By midday Karl had done well. His knapsack was so heavy that he had trouble carrying it. He lay in a trench which was overgrown with a rich variety of weeds and grasses and smelled delicious. The early autumn day was warm and Karl had been amazed to see a pair of hares. He had killed one, but the other had fled. He was hoping it would reappear. When he had it, he would go home. He had not eaten that morning and was both tired and hungry.

The rims of the glasses were beginning to irritate his eyes when he caught a movement to the South and adjusted the focus quickly. At first he was disappointed. It wasn't the hare, only a man.

The man was running. Sometimes he fell down, but picked himself up again immediately, running on. His back was bowed and he waved his arms loosely as he ran. Karl could now see that he was in uniform. The uniform was probably grey. It was covered in mud. The man was hatless and had no weapons. Karl hadn't seen a soldier in this part of the world for well over a year. He had heard the gunfire, as had everyone else, but otherwise his particular village had seen no action for ages.

The German soldier came closer. He was unshaven. His eyes were red. He gasped as he moved. He seemed to be running away. Surely the Allies had not broken through the German line? Karl had been certain it would hold forever. It seemed to have been holding for almost as long as he could remember. The thought unsettled him. He had been happy with the status quo and wasn't sure if he looked forward to any change.

More likely the German soldier was a deserter. A silly place to desert, round here. Still . . .

Karl yawned. Another quarter of an hour and he'd leave. He hung his fieldglasses round his neck and picked up his rifle. He sighted down the barrel, aiming at the German soldier. He pretended he was in the war and that this was an attack on his trench. He cocked the bolt of the rifle. There were thousands of them attacking now. He squeezed the trigger.

Although he was surprised when the German threw up his arms and shouted (he could hear the shout from where he lay) he did not regret his action. He raised his fieldglasses. The bullet had struck the soldier in the stomach. A careless shot. But then he hadn't been aiming properly. The soldier fell down in the long grass and Karl saw it waving. He frowned. The waving stopped. He wondered whether to go home or whether to cross the field and have a look at the soldier. Morally, he should look at the soldier. After all, it was the first time he had killed a human being. He shrugged and left his bag of mixed meat where it was. The soldier might have something useful on him, anyway.

With his rifle over his shoulder, he began to plod towards the spot where his man had fallen.

— *Is it morning yet? asks Karl, yawning.*
— *No. A long time until morning, Karl.*
— *The night seems to be lasting forever.*
— *Aren't you glad?*
He feels a strong hand in his crotch. It squeezes him gently but firmly. Karl's lips part a little.
— *Yes, says Karl, I'm glad.*

You are a white man in a town where the people are predominantly black.

Because of indignities and insufficient representation of their cause, the black people, militant and angry, seize control of the town.

They are met with violence from some of the whites and they respond in turn, lynching two white officials against whom they have particular grievances.

But now the people have become a mob and are out for white blood. The mob is approaching your part of the town, smashing and burning and beating whites. Some of the whites have been beaten to death.

You cannot contact your black friends and ask for their help because you don't know exactly where they are.

Would you hide in the house and hope that the mob didn't bother you?

Would you try to take your chances on the street and hope to find a black friend who would vouch for you?

Would you go to the aid of other white people defending themselves against the mob? Would you then try to make everyone calm down?

Or would you simply help your fellow white people kill the black people attacking them?

Or would you join the black people attacking the whites and hope to win acceptance that way?

9

The Downline to Kiev: 1920: Shuffling Along

Official verification came to hand yesterday of the report recently published of the ex-Tsar's violent end at Ekaterinburg at the hands of his Red Guards. The message has been transmitted as follows through the wireless stations of the Russian Government:

Recently Ekaterinburg, the capital of the Red Ural, was seriously threatened by the approach of the Czecho-Slovak bands. At the same time a counter-revolutionary conspiracy was discovered, having for its object the wresting of the ex-Tsar from the hands of the Council's authority by armed force. In view of this fact the Council decided to shoot the ex-Tsar. This decision was carried out on July 16. The wife and son of Romanoff have been sent to a place of security. Documents concerning the conspiracy, which were discovered, have been forwarded to Moscow by a special messenger. It had been recently decided to bring the ex-Tsar before a tribunal to be tried for his crimes against the people and only later occurrences led to delay in adopting this course. The Russian Executive Council accept the decision of the Rural Regional Council as being regular. The Central Executive Committee has now at its disposal extremely important material and documents concerning the Nicholas Romanoff affair – his own diary, which he kept almost to the last day, diaries of his wife and children, his correspondence, amongst which are letters by Gregory Rasputin to Romanoff and his family. All these materials will be examined and published in the near future.

NEWS OF THE WORLD, *Sunday, July 21, 1918.*

Seated before the mirror, Karl examines his flesh. Neither the harsh neon light over the mirror, nor the mirror itself, are flattering. Karl pouts his lips and rolls his eyes.

– I don't think you're a Nigerian at all, now. Your accent changes all the time.

– We all change our accents to suit our circumstances. In the mirror their eyes meet. Karl feels cold.

We are all victims.

He is fourteen. His mother and his father were killed in an explosion in a cafe in Bobrinskaya.

Karl's friend puts friendly hands on Karl's shoulders. – What would you like to do now?

He is fourteen. Sitting on a flat car, hanging on for dear life as the train roars across the plain. The plain is dead. It consists of nothing but the blackened stalks of what was once wheat. The wheat has been deliberately burned.

The sky is huge and empty.

Karl shivers.

– Any ideas?

The train moves to meet the sullen bank of grey cloud on the horizon. It is like the end of the world. The train carries death. It goes to find more death. That is its cargo, its destiny.

At several points on the train – on the locomotive bellowing ahead, on the rocking carriages, the bucking open trucks – black flags flap like the wings of settling crows.

It is the Ukraine.

And Karl shivers.

KARL WAS FOURTEEN. His mother and father had been thirty-five when they were killed by the bomb. They came from Kiev but had been driven out during one of the pogroms. They had thought it safer to stay with their relatives in Bobrinskaya. Someone had let a bomb off in a cafe and Karl had gone to Alexandria where he had met the army of Makhno, the Anarchist. He had joined that army. He had been in several battles since then and now he had a machine gun of his own to look after. He loved the machine gun. He had secured the stand to the flat car with big horse-shoe nails. It was an English machine gun, a Lewis. His greatcoat was English, too. It was leather and had a special pocket in the front shaped like a revolver. During their last battle, near Golta, he had managed to acquire a revolver. They had been beaten at that battle. They were now making for Kiev because the railway line direct to Alexandria had been blown up to cut off their retreat. Makhno's black banners flew everywhere on the train. Some of the banners bore his slogan: Anarchy Breeds Order. But most were plain. Makhno was in a bad mood since Golta.

Over the rattle of the train and the roar of the locomotive came the sounds of laughter, of song, of an accordion's whine. Makhno's army lounged on every available surface. Young men, mainly, their clothes were evidence of a hundred successful raids. One wore a tall silk hat decorated with streaming red and black ribbons. His body was swathed in a sleeveless fur coat with the skirt hacked off to give his legs freedom. He wore green Cossack breeches tucked into red leather boots. Over his coat were criss-crossed four bandoliers of bullets. In his hands was a rifle which, intermittently, he would fire into the air, laughing all the time. At his belt was a curved sabre and stuck in the belt were a Mauser automatic pistol and a Smith and Wesson .45 revolver. Bottles were passed from hand to hand as they thundered along. The young man in the top hat flung back his head and poured wine over his bearded face and down his throat, breaking into song as the accordion began to play the army's familiar melody, "Arise young men!" Karl himself joined in with the sad, bold last lines, "Who lies under the green sward?" sang the man in the top hat. "We heroes of Makhno," sang Karl, "saddle rugs for shrouds."

There was a great cheer and peaked caps, sheepskin hats, derby hats, stocking caps and the caps of a dozen different regiments were waved or thrown through the steam from the engine. Karl was proud to be of this reckless company which cared nothing for death and very little for life. The cause for which they fought might be doomed but what did it matter? The human race was doomed. They at least would have made their gesture.

There was not a man on the train who was not festooned with weapons. Sabres and rifles and pistols were common to all. Some sported ornate antique weapons, broadswords, officers' dress swords, pistols inlaid with gold, silver and mother-o'-pearl. They wore boaters, solar topees, extravagant German helmets, wide-brimmed felt hats, panamas and every variety of clothing. Near Karl and manning one of the other machine guns, a fat Georgian was stripped to the waist, wearing only a pair of gentleman's blue riding breeches and boots decorated with silver thread. Around his neck he had wound a long feather boa. He was hatless, but had on a pair of smoked glasses with gold rims. At his belt were two military holsters containing matched-revolvers. The Georgian claimed that they had belonged to the Emperor himself. Sharing a bottle with the Georgian was a sailor from Odessa, his vest open to the navel, displaying a torso completely covered in pink and blue tattoos showing dragons, swords and half-dressed ladies all mixed up together. The freshest of the tattoos ran across his breastbone, a Nihilist slogan – Death to Life. A boy, younger than Karl, wearing a torn and bloodstained surplice, clutching a cooked chicken in one hand, jumped down from the top of the box-car behind them and swayed towards the sailor, offering him half the chicken in exchange for the rest of the wine. In his other hand he held an enormous butcher's cleaver. The boy was already nine parts drunk.

The train hooted.

Balancing on the carriage ahead, an old man, with a student cap perched on his white hair hooted back. He steadied himself by means of a Cossack lance around which was tied a torn black skirt. Painted on the skirt was a yellow sunrise. The old man hooted again, before falling on his side and rolling dangerously close to the edge of the roof. The lance remained where he had stuck it. The old man lost his cap and began to laugh. The train took a bend. The old man fell off. Karl saluted the tumbling figure as it disappeared down a bank.

On the curve, Karl could see the front section of the train where Nestor Makhno himself sat. The flat-wagons on both sides of him were piled with gun-carriages, their dirty steel and brasswork shining dully beneath a sun which now only made occasional appearances through the looming clouds. A truck near to the engine was full of shaggy horses, their backs covered by Jewish prayer-shawls in place of blankets. Makhno's chosen Heroes sat all around their leader, their feet dangling over the sides of the wagons, but none sat near him. Karl had an impression of nothing but legs. There were legs in riding boots, legs in puttees made from silk dresses or red plush or green baize ripped from a billiard table, feet in yellow silk slippers with velvet pompoms bouncing on them, in felt shoes, in laced boots, in sandals and in brogues, or some completely naked, scratched, red, horny, dirty. No songs came from Makhno's guard. They were probably all too drunk to sing.

On Makhno's wagon a huge, gleaming black landau had been anchored. The landau's door was decorated with the gilded coat of arms of some dead aristocrat. The upholstery was a rich crimson morocco leather. The shafts of the landau stuck up into the air and on each shaft flapped a black banner of Anarchy. On each corner of the wagon was placed a highly-polished machine gun and at each machine gun squatted a man in a white Cossack cap and a black leather greatcoat. These four were not drunk. Makhno himself was probably not drunk. He lay against the leather cushions of the landau and laughed to himself, tossing a revolver high into the air and catching it again, his feet in their shining black boots crossed indolently on the coach box.

Nestor Makhno was dying. Karl realised it suddenly. The

man was small and sickly. His face was the grey face of death. The black Cossack hat and the gay, embroidered Cossack jacket he wore only served to emphasise the pallor of his features. Over his forehead hung a damp fringe of hair which made him look a little like some pictures of Napoleon. And his eyes were alive. Even from where he sat Karl could see the eyes – blazing with a wild and malevolent misery.

Nestor Makhno tossed the revolver up again and caught it. He tossed it and caught it again.

Karl saw that they were nearing a station. The train howled.

The platform was deserted. If there were passengers waiting for a train, they were hiding. People normally hid when Makhno's army came through. Karl grinned to himself. This was not an age in which the timid could survive.

The train slowed as it approached the station. Did Makhno intend to stop for some reason?

And then, incongruously, a guard appeared on the platform. He was dressed in the uniform of the railway line and he held a green flag in his right hand. What a fool he was, thought Karl, still sticking to the rule book while the world was being destroyed around him.

The guard raised his left hand to his head in a shaky salute. There was a terrified grin on his face, an imploring, placatory grin.

The front part of the train was by now passing through the station. Karl saw Nestor Makhno catch his revolver and cock it. Then, casually, as his landau came level with the guard, Makhno fired. He did not even bother to aim. He had hardly glanced at the guard. Perhaps he had not really intended to hit the man. But the guard fell, stumbling backwards on buckling legs and then crumpling against the wall of his office, his whole body shuddering as he dropped his flag and grasped at his neck. His chest heaved and blood vomited from between his lips.

Karl laughed. He swung his machine-gun round and jerked the trigger. The gun began to sing. The bullets smashed into the walls and made the body of the guard dance for a few seconds. Karl saw that the placatory smile was still on the dead man's face. He pulled the trigger again and raked the whole station as they went through. Glass smashed, a sign fell down, someone screamed.

The name of the station was Pomoshnaya.

Karl turned to the fat Georgian who had opened a fresh bottle of vodka and was drinking from it in great gulps. He had hardly noticed Karl's action. Karl tapped him on the shoulder.

"Hey, old Pyat – where the hell is Pomoshnaya?"

The Georgian shrugged and offered Karl the bottle. He was too fuddled to understand the question.

The station was disappearing behind them. Soon it had vanished.

The tattooed sailor, his arm around a snub-nosed girl with cropped hair, a Mauser in her hand, took the bottle from the Georgian and placed it against the girl's thin lips. "Drink up," he said. He peered at Karl. "What was that, youngster?"

Karl tried to repeat his question, but the train entered a tunnel and thick smoke filled their lungs, stung their eyes and they could see nothing. Everyone began to cough and to curse.

"It doesn't matter," said Karl.

– You're still looking a bit pale, says Karl's friend, fingering his own ebony skin. – Maybe you could do with another bath?

Karl shakes his head. – It'll be hard enough getting this lot off. I've got to leave here sometime, you know. It's going to be embarrassing.

– Only if you let it be. Brazen it out. After all, you're not the only one, are you?

Karl giggles. – I bet you say that to all the boys.

You have been told that you have at most a year to live. Would you decide to spend that year:

(a) enjoying every possible pleasure?
(b) doing charitable works?
(c) in some quiet retreat, relishing the simpler pleasures of life?
(d) trying to accomplished one big thing that you will be remembered for in times to come?
(e) putting all your resources into finding a cure for the illness you have?

or would you simply kill yourself and get the whole thing over with?

10

Hitting the High Spots
on W. Fifty-Six:
1929: Recognition

Trapped at sea in a violent thunder storm, the U.S.S.
Akron, largest and finest dirigible airship in the
world, crashed off the Barnegat Lightship at 12:30
o'clock this morning with 77 officers and men
aboard. Among them was Rear Admiral William A.
Moffett, chief of the Bureau of Aeronautics.

Only four of the 77 were known to have been
saved at 5 o'clock this morning. At that time the
wreckage of the stricken airship was out of sight in
the storm and darkness from the German oil tanker
Phoebus, which first reported the catastrophe. A
northwest wind blowing about 45 miles an hour was
blowing the wreckage off shore and made rescue
operations doubly difficult.

No hint of the cause of the disaster was contained
in the fragmentary and frequently confusing reports
received from the *Phoebus*, but it was considered
highly likely that the great airship was struck by
lightning.

THE NEW YORK TIMES, *April 4, 1933*.

*– You were bound to get depressed after all that excite-
ment, says Karl's friend. – What about some coffee? Or
would you rather I sent down for some more champagne?
He grins, making an expansive gesture.*

– *Name your poison!*

Karl sighs and chews at his thumbnail. His eyes are hooded. He won't look at the black man.

– *All right, then how can I cheer you up?*

– *You could fuck off,* says Karl.

– *Take it easy, Karl.*

– *You could fuck off.*

– *What good would that do?*

– *I didn't know you were interested in doing good.*

– *Where did you get that idea? Don't you feel more a person now than you felt before you came with me through the door? More real?*

– *Maybe that's the trouble.*

– *You don't like reality?*

– *Yes, maybe that's it.*

– *Well, that isn't my problem.*

– *No.*

– *It's your problem.*

– *Yes.*

– *Oh, come on now! You're starting a new life and you can't manage even a tiny smile!*

– *I'm not your slave,* says Karl. *I don't have to do everything you say.*

– *Who said you had to? Me?* The black man laughs deridingly. – *Did I say that?*

– *I thought that was the deal.*

– *Deal? Now you're being obscure. I thought you wanted some fun.*

Karl is fifteen. Quite a little man now.

– *Fuck off,* he says. – *Leave me alone.*

– *In my experience,* the black man sits down beside him, *that's what people always say when they think they're not getting enough attention. It's a challenge, in a way. 'Leave me alone.'*

– *Maybe you're right.*

– *Darling, I'm not often wrong.* The black man once again puts his arm around Karl's shoulders.

Karl is fifteen and in his own way pretty good looking. He's dating the sweetest little tomato in the school.

– Oh, Jesus!
Karl begins to weep.
– Now that's enough of that, says his friend.

Karl was fifteen. His Mom was forty. His Dad was forty-two. His Dad had done all right for himself in his business and just recently had become President of one of the biggest investment trusts in the nation. He had, to celebrate, increased Karl's allowance at his fifteenth birthday and turned a blind eye when Karl borrowed his mother's car when he went out on a date. Karl was a big boy for his age and looked older than fifteen.

In his new tuxedo and with his hair gleaming with oil, Karl could have passed for twenty easily. That was probably why Nancy Goldmann was so willing to let him take her out.

As they left the movie theatre (*Gold Diggers of Broadway*), he whistled one of the tunes from the film while he gathered his courage together to suggest to Nancy what he had been meaning to suggest all evening.

Nancy put her arm through his and saved him the worst part: "Where to now?" she asked.

"There's a speakeasy I know on West Fifty Six." He guided her across the street while the cars honked on all sides. It was getting dark and the lights were coming on all down Forty Second Street. "What do you say, Nancy?" They reached his car. It was a new Ford Coupe. His Dad had a Cadillac limousine which he hoped to borrow by the time he was sixteen. He opened the door for Nancy.

"A speakeasy, Karl? I don't know . . ." She hesitated before getting into the car. He glanced away from her calves. His eyes would keep going to them. It was the short, fluffy skirt. You could almost see through it.

"Aw, come on, Nancy. Are you bored with speakeasies? Is that it?"

She laughed. "No! Will it be dangerous? Gangsters and bootleggers and shooting and stuff?"

"It'll be the dullest place in the world. But we can get a drink there." He hoped she would have a drink, then she
111

might do more than hold his hand and kiss him on the way home. He had only a vague idea of what "more" meant. "If you want one, of course."

"Well, maybe just one."

He could see that Nancy was excited.

All the way up to W.56th Street she chattered beside him, talking about the movie mostly. He could tell that she was unconsciously seeing herself as Ann Pennington. Well, he didn't mind that. He grinned to himself as he parked the car. Taking his hat and his evening coat from the back, he walked round and opened the door for Nancy. She really was beautiful. And she was warm.

They crossed Seventh Avenue and were nearly bowled over by a man in a straw hat who mumbled an apology and hurried on. Karl thought it was a bit late in the year to be wearing a straw hat. He shrugged and then, on impulse, leaned forward and kissed Nancy's cheek. Not only didn't she resist, she blew him a kiss back and laughed her lovely trilling laugh. "Did anyone ever tell you you looked like Rudy Vallee?" she said.

"Lots of people." He smirked in a comic way and made her laugh again.

They came to a gaudy neon sign which flashed on and off. It showed a pink pyramid, a blue and green dancing girl, a white camel. It was called the Casa Blanca.

"Shall we?" said Karl, opening the door for her.

"This is a restaurant."

"Just wait and see!"

They checked their hats and coats and were shown by an ingratiating little waiter to a table some distance from the stand where a band was backing someone who looked and sounded almost exactly like Janet Gaynor. She was even singing Keep Your Sunny Side Up.

"What happens next?" said Nancy. She was beginning to look disappointed.

The waiter brought the menus and bowed. Karl had been told what to say by his friend Paul who had recommended the place. "Could we have some soft drinks, please?" he said.

"Certainly, sir. What kind?"

"Uh – the strong kind, please." Karl looked significantly at the waiter.

"Yes, sir." The waiter went away again.

Karl held Nancy's hand. She responded with a funny little spasm and grinned at him. "What are you going to eat?"

"Oh, anything. Steak Diane. I'm mad about Steak Diane."

"Me too." Under the table, his knee touched Nancy's and she didn't move away. Of course, there was always the chance that she thought his knee was a table leg or something. Then, when she looked at him, she moved her chin up in a way that told him she knew it was his knee. He swallowed hard. The waiter arrived with the drinks, He ordered two Steak Dianes "and all the trimmings". He lifted his glass and toasted Nancy. They sipped together.

"They've put a lot of lemon in it," said Nancy. "I guess they have to. In case of a raid or something."

"That's it," said Karl, fingering his bow tie.

He saw his father just as his father saw him. He wondered if his father would take the whole thing in good part. The band struck up and a couple of thinly dressed lady dancers began to Charleston. He saw that the lady dining with his father was not his mother. In fact she looked too young to be anybody's mother, in spite of the make-up. Karl's father left his place and came over to Karl's table. Mr. Glogauer nodded at Nancy and glared at Karl. "Get out of here at once and don't tell your mother you saw me here tonight. Who told you about this place?" He had to speak loudly because the band was now in full swing. A lot of people were clapping in time to the music.

"I just knew about it, Dad."

"Did you. Do you come here often, then? Do you know what kind of a place this is? It's a haunt of gangsters, immoral women, all kinds of riffraff!"

Karl looked at his father's young friend.

"That young lady is the daughter of a business associate," said Mr. Glogauer. "I brought her here because she

113

said she wanted to see some New York nightlife. It is not the place for a boy of fifteen!"

Nancy got up. "I think I'll get somebody to call me a cab," she said. She paused, then took her drink and swallowed it all down. Karl ran after her and caught her at the checking desk. "There's another place I know, Nancy," he said.

She stopped, pulling on her hat and giving him a calculating look. Then her expression softened. "We could go back to my place? My Mom and Pop are out."

"Oh, great!"

On the way back to Nancy's place in the car she put her arms round his neck and nibbled his ear and ruffled his hair.

"You're just a little boy at heart, aren't you?" she said.

His knees shook. He had heard that line earlier tonight and he could guess what it meant.

He knew he would always remember this day in September.

— Thanks. Karl accepts the cup of coffee his friend hands him. — How long have I been asleep?

— Not long.

Karl remembers their scene. He wishes it hadn't happened. He was behaving like some little fairy, all temperament and flounce. Homosexual relationships didn't have to be like that now. It was normal, after all. Between normal people, he thought. That was the difference. He looked at his friend. The man was sitting naked on the edge of a chest of drawers, swinging his leg lazily as he smoked a cigarette. His body really was beautiful. It was attractive in itself. It was very masculine. Oddly, it made Karl feel more masculine, too. That was what he found strange. He had thought things would be different. He kept being reminded of some quality he had always felt in his father when his father had been at home.

— Did you dream anything? asked the black man.

— I don't remember.

114

What Would You Do? (10)

You are married with a family and you live in a small apartment in the city, reasonably close to your work.

You learn that your mother has become very ill and can no longer look after herself.

You hate the idea of her coming to live with you in your already cramped conditions, particularly since she is not a very nice old woman and tends to make the children nervous and your wife tense. Your mother's house is larger, but in a part of the world which depresses you and which is also a long way from your work. Yet you have always sworn that you will not let her go into an Old People's Home. You know it would cause her considerable misery. Any other decision, however, would mean you changing your way of life quite radically.

Would you sell your mother's house and use the money to buy a larger flat in your own area? Or would you move away to a completely different area, perhaps somewhere in the country, and look for a new job?

Or would you decide, after all, that it would be best for everyone if she did go into a Retirement Home?

11

Shanghai Sally: 1932: Problems of Diplomacy

In Shanghai is one of the most extraordinarily gruesome sights in the world. I have never seen anything to approach it. Parts of Chapei and Hongkew, where fighting was hottest, are in ruins paralleling those of the Western Front in France. The Japanese looted this area, which comprises several square miles, not merely of furniture, valuables, and household possessions, but of every nail, every window wire, every screw, bolt, nut, or key, every infinitesimal piece of metal they could lay hands on. Houses were ripped to pieces, then the whole region set on fire. No one lives in this charred ruin now. No one could. The Japanese have, however, maintained street lighting; the lighted avenues protrude through an area totally black, totally devoid of human life, like phosphorescent fingers poking into a grisly void.

What is known as the Garden Bridge separates this Japanese-occupied area with one rim of the International Settlement proper. Barbed wire and sandbags protect it. Japanese sentries representing army, navy, and police stand at one end. British sentries are at the other. I have seen these tall Englishmen go white with rage as the Japanese, a few feet away, kicked coolies or slapped old men. The Japanese have life-and-death power over any-

116

one in their area. Chinese, passing the Japanese sentries, have to bow ceremoniously, and doff their hats. Yet the Japanese – at the same time they may playfully prod a man across the bridge with their bayonets – say that they are in China to make friends of the Chinese people!

Lest it be thought that I exaggerate I append the following Reuter dispatch from Shanghai of date March 30, 1938:

"Feeling is running high in British military circles here today as a result of an incident which occurred this morning on a bridge over the Soochow Creek ... Japanese soldiers set upon and beat an old Chinese man who happened to be on the bridge, and then threw him over into the water. The whole action was in full view of sentries of the Durhams, who were on duty, at one end of the bridge. The British soldiers, unable to leave their posts, were compelled helplessly to watch the old man drown, while the Japanese soldiers laughed and cheered."

INSIDE ASIA, by John Gunter
Hamish Hamilton, 1939.

– We protect ourselves in so many foolish ways, says Karl's friend. – But let the defences drop and we discover that we are much happier.

– I don't feel much happier.

– Not at present, perhaps. Freedom, after all, takes some getting used to.

– I don't feel free.

– Not yet.

– There is no such thing as freedom.

– Of course there is! It's often hard to assimilate a new idea, I know.

– Your ideas don't seem particularly new.

– Oh, you just haven't understood yet, that's all!

Karl is sixteen. Shanghai is the largest city in China. It is one of the most exciting and romantic cities in the world. His mother and father came here to live two years ago.

There are no taxes in Shanghai. Great ships stand in the harbour. War ships stand a few miles out to sea. Anything can happen in Shanghai.

– Why do people always need a philosophy to justify their lusts? Karl says spitefully. – What's so liberating about sex of any kind?

– It isn't just the sex.

Black smoke boils over the city from the north. People are complaining.

– No, it's power.

– Oh, come, come, Karl! Take it easy!

Karl Glogauer is sixteen. Although a German by birth, he attends the British school because it is considered to be the best.

– Who do you like best! asks Karl. – Men or women?

– I love everyone, Karl.

KARL WAS SIXTEEN. His mother was forty-two. His father was fifty. They all lived in the better part of Shanghai and enjoyed many benefits they would not have been able to afford in Munich.

Having dined with his father at the German Club, Karl, feeling fat and contented, ambled through the revolving glass doors into the bright sunshine and noisy bustle of the Bund, Shanghai's main street and the city's heart. The wide boulevard fronted the harbour and offered him a familiar view of junks and steamers and even a few yachts with crisp, white sails, sailing gently up towards the sea. As he creased the crown of his cream-coloured hat he noticed with dissatisfaction that there was a spot of dark grease on the cuff of his right sleeve. He adjusted the hat on his head and with the fingers of both hands turned down the brim a little. Then he looked out over the Bund to see if his mother had arrived yet. She had arranged to meet him at three o'clock and take him home in the car. He searched the mass of traffic but couldn't see her. There were trams and buses and trucks and cars, rickshaws and pedicabs, transport of every possible description, but no Rolls-Royce. He was content to wait and watch the passing throng.

Shanghai must be the one place in the world where one never tired of the view. He could see people on the Bund of virtually every race on Earth: Chinese from all parts of China, from beautifully elegant businessmen in well-tailored Europeans suits, mandarins in flowing silks, singing girls in slit skirts, flashily dressed gangster types, sailors and soldiers to the poorest coolies in smocks or loin-cloths. As well as the Chinese, there were Indian merchants and clerks, French industrialists with their wives, German ship-brokers, Dutch, Swedish, English and American factory-owners or their employees, all moving along in the twin tides that swept back and forth along the Bund. As well as the babble of a hundred languages, there was the rich, satisfying smell of Shanghai, a mixture of human sweat and machine oil, of spices and drugs and stimulants, of cooking food and exhaust fumes. Horns barked, beggars whined, street-sellers shouted their wares. Shanghai.

Karl smiled. If it were not for the present trouble the Japanese were having in their sector of the International District, Shanghai would offer a young man the best of all possible worlds. For entertainment there were the cinemas, theatres and clubs, the brothels and dance-halls along the Szechwan Road. You could buy anything you wanted – a piece of jade, a bale of silk, embroideries, fine porcelain, imports from Paris, New York and London, a child of any age or sex, a pipe of opium, a limousine with bullet-proof glass, the most exotic meal in the world, the latest books in any language, instruction in any religion or aspect of mysticism. Admittedly there was poverty (he had heard than an average of 29,000 people starved to death on the streets of Shanghai every year) but it was a price that had to be paid for so much colour and beauty and experience. In the two years that he had been here he had managed to sample only a few of Shanghai's delights and, as he neared manhood, the possibilities of what he could do became wider and wider. No one could have a better education than to be brought up in Shanghai.

He saw the Rolls pull in to the kerb and he waved. His mother, wearing one of her least extravagant hats, leaned out of the window and waved back. He sprang down the steps and pushed his way through the crowd until he got to the car. The Chinese chauffeur, whose name Karl could never remember and whom he always called "Hank", got out and opened the door, saluting him. Karl gave him a friendly grin. He stepped into the car and stretched out beside his mother, kissing her lightly on the cheek. "Lovely perfume," he said. He flattered her as a matter of habit, but she was always pleased. It hardly occurred to him to dislike anything she chose to do, wear or say. She was his mother, after all. He was her son.

"Oh, Karl, it's been terrible today." Frau Glogauer was Hungarian and spoke German, as she spoke French and English, with a soft, pretty accent. She was very popular with the gentlemen in all the best European circles of the city. "I meant to do much more shopping, but there wasn't time. The traffic! That's why I was late, darling."

"Only five minutes, Mama." Karl looked at his Swiss watch. "I always give you at least half-an-hour, you know that. Do you want to finish your shopping before we go home?" They lived in the fashionable Frenchtown area to the west, not too far from the Race Course, in a large Victorian Gothic house which Karl's father had purchased very reasonably from the American who had previously owned it.

His mother shook her head. "No. No. I get irritable if I can't do everything at my own pace and it's impossible this afternoon. I wish those Japanese would hurry up and restore order. A handful of bandits can't cause that much trouble, surely? I'm sure if the Japanese had a free hand, the whole city would be better run. We ought to put them in charge."

"There'd be fewer people to manage," said Karl dryly. "I'm afraid I don't like them awfully. They're a bit too heavy-handed in their methods, if you ask me."

"Do the Chinese understand any other methods?" His mother hated being contradicted. She shrugged and pouted out of the window.

"But perhaps you're right," he conceded.

"Well, see for yourself," she said, gesturing into the street. It was true that the usual dense mass of traffic was if anything denser, was moving more slowly, with less order, hampered by even more pedestrians than was normal at this hour. Karl didn't like the look of a lot of them. Really villainous wretches in their grubby smocks and head-rags. "It's chaos!" his mother continued. "We're having to go half-way round the city to get home."

"I suppose it's the refugees from the Japanese quarters," said Karl. "You could blame the Japs for the delays, too, mother."

"I blame the Chinese," she said firmly. "In the end, it always comes down to them. They are the most inefficient people on the face of the Earth. And lazy!"

Karl laughed. "And devious. They're terrible scamps, I'll agree. But don't you love them, really? What would Shanghai be without them?"

"Orderly," she said, but she was forced to smile back at him, making fun at herself for her outburst, "and clean. They run all the vice-rings, you know. The opium-dens, the dance-halls . . ."

"That's what I meant!"

They laughed together.

The car moved forward a few more inches. The chauffeur sounded the horn.

Frau Glogauer hissed in despair and flung herself back against the upholstery, her gloved fingers tapping the arm of the seat.

Karl pulled the speaking tube towards him. "Could you try another way, Hank? This seems impassable."

The Chinese, in his neat grey uniform, nodded but did nothing. There were carts and rickshaws packing the street in front of him and a large truck blocking his way back. "We could walk," said Karl.

His mother ignored him, her lips pursed. A moment later she took out her handbag and opened the flap so that she could look into the mirror set inside it. She brushed with her little finger at her right eyelid. It was a gesture of withdrawal. Karl stared out of the window. He could see the skyscrapers of the Bund looming close behind them still. They had not gone far. He studied the shops on both sides. For all that the street was crowded, nobody seemed to be doing much business. He watched a fat Indian in a linen suit and a white turban pause outside a shop selling the newspapers of a dozen countries. The Indian picked his nose as he studied the papers, then he selected an American pulp magazine from another rack and paid the proprietor. Rolling the magazine up, the Indian walked rapidly away. It seemed to Karl that some more mysterious transaction must have taken place. But then every transaction seemed like that in Shanghai.

The Rolls rolled a few more feet. Then the chauffeur saw an opening in a sidestreet and turned down it. He managed to get half-way before a night-soil cart – the "honey-carts" as the Chinese called them – got in his way and he was forced to brake quite sharply. The driver of the cart pretended not to notice the car. One wheel of his cart mounted the sidewalk as he squeezed past. Then they were able to drive into the sidestreet which was barely wide enough to accommodate the big Phantom.

"At least we're moving," said Frau Glogauer, putting her compact back into her bag and closing the clasp with a snap. "Where are we?"

"We're going all round the world," said Karl. "The river's just ahead, I think. Is that a bridge?" He craned forward, trying to get his bearings. "Now that must be north . . . My God!"

"What?"

"Chapei. They must have set fire to it. The smoke. I thought it was clouds."

"Will it mean trouble – here, I mean?" asked his mother, taking hold of his arm.

He shook his head. "I've no idea. We're pretty close to the Japanese concession now. Maybe we should go back and speak to Father?"

She was silent. She liked to make the decisions. But the political situation had never interested her. She always found it boring. Now she had no information on which to base a decision. "Yes, I suppose so," she said reluctantly. "That was gunfire, wasn't it?"

"It was something exploding." Karl suddenly felt an intense hatred for the Japanese. With all their meddling, they could ruin Shanghai for everybody. He took up the speaking tube. "Back to the Bund, Hank, as soon as you can get out of here."

They entered a wider thoroughfare and Karl saw the crowds part as if swept back by invisible walls. Through the corridor thus created a Chinese youth came running. Hank had pulled out into the street and now the car was blocking the youth's progress.

Behind the youth came three little Japanese policemen with clubs and pistols in their hands. They were chasing him. The youth did not appear to see the car and he struck it in the way that a moth might strike a screen door. He fell backwards and then tried to scramble up. He was completely dazed. Karl wondered what to do.

The Japense policemen flung themselves onto the youth, their clubs rising and falling.

Karl started to wind down the window. "Hey!"

His mother buried her face in his shoulder. He saw a smear of powder on his lapel. "Oh, Karl!"

He put his arm around his mother's warm body. The smell of her perfume seemed even stronger. He saw blood well out of the bruises on the Chinese boy's face and back. Hank was trying to turn the car into the main street. A tug went past on the river, its funnel belching white smoke which contrasted sharply with the oily black smoke rising over Chapei. It was strange how peaceful the rest of the tall city looked. The New York of the Orient.

The clubs continued to rise and fall. His mother snuffled in his shoulder. Karl turned his eyes away from the sight. The car began to reverse a fraction. There was a tap on the window. One of the Japanese policemen stood there, bowing and smiling and saluting with his bloody club. He made some apology in Japanese and grinned widely, shaking his free hand as if to say "Such things happen in even the best-run city." Karl leant over and wound the window right up.

The car pulled away from the scene. He didn't look back.

As they drove towards the Bund again, Karl's mother sniffed, straightened up and fumbled in her handbag for a handkerchief. "Oh, that awful man," she said. "And those policemen! They must have been drunk."

Karl was happy to accept this explanation. "Of course," he said. "They were drunk."

The car stopped.

– *There is certainly something secure, says Karl, about a world which excludes women. Which is not to say that I deny their charms and their virtues. But I can understand, suddenly, one of the strong appeals of the homosexual world.*

– *Now you're thinking of substituting one narrow world for another, warns his friend. – I spoke earlier of broadening your experience. That's quite different.*

– *What if the person isn't up to being broadened? I mean, we all have a limited capacity for absorbing experience, surely? I could be, as it were, naturally narrow.*

Karl feels euphoric. He smiles slowly.

– *No one but a moron could be that, says the black man, just a trifle prudishly.*

What Would You Do? (11)

A girl you know has become pregnant.

You are almost certainly the father.

The girl is not certain whether she wants the baby or not. She asks you to help her to decide.

Would you try to convince her to have an abortion?

Would you try to convince her to have the baby?

Would you offer to support her, if she had the baby?

Would you deny that the baby was yours and have nothing further to do with the girl?

If she decided to have an abortion and it had to be done privately, would you offer to pay the whole cost?

Would you tell her that the decision was entirely up to her and refuse to be drawn into any discussion?

12

Memories of Berlin: 1935: Dusty

King Alexander of Yugoslavia was assassinated at Marseilles yesterday. M. Barthou, the French Foreign Minister, who had gone to the port to greet the King, was also murdered.

The assassin jumped on the running board of the car in which the King, who had only just landed, was driving with M. Barthou, General Georges, and Admiral Berthelot, and fired a series of shots. The General and the Admiral were both wounded. The murderer, believed to be a Croat, was killed by the guard.

King Alexander was on his way to Paris for a visit of great political importance. It was to have been the occasion of an attempt to find means, through French mediation, of improving relations between Yugoslavia, the ally of France, and Italy, as preliminary to a Franco-Italian rapprochement.

THE TIMES *October 10, 1934.*

A policy of keeping the United States "unentangled and free" was announced here today by President Roosevelt in his first public utterance recognizing the gravity of war abroad ...

The general advance of the Italian armies from Eritrea has begun. At dawn today 20,000 men in four columns crossed the Mareb River which forms the Ethiopian boundary. Groups of light tanks operating ahead covered the crossing. Airplanes hovered overhead and long range guns fired occasional shells to

discourage opposition. Italian planes bombed Adowa
and Adigrat ...

THE NEW YORK TIMES, *October 2 and 3, 1935.*

The Italian government is capable of almost any kind
of treason".

ADOLPH HITLER, *August 9, 1943.*

*He looks up into the cloudy eyes of his friend. You
seem quite pale, he says. – Why doesn't anything happen?
Karl wipes his lips.*

*–That's none of your business, says the black man. I feel
like a drink. Do you want one? He turns and goes to the
table where the waiter has arranged a variety of drinks.
– What do you like?*

– I don't drink much. A lemonade will do.

– A glass of wine?

– All right.

*Karl accepts the glass of red wine. He holds it up to a
beam of moonlight.– I wish I could help you, he says.*

– Don't worry about that.

*– If you say so. Karl sits down on the edge of the bed,
swinging his legs and sipping his wine. – Do you think I'm
unimaginative?*

– I suppose you are. But that's nothing to do with it.

– Maybe that's why I never made much of a painter.

– There are lots of different kinds of imagination.

*– Yes. It's a funny thing. Imagination is man's greatest
strength and yet it's also his central weakness. Imagination
was a survival trait at first, but when it becomes over-
developed it destroys him, like the tusks of a mammoth
growing into its own eyes. Imagination, in my opinion, is
being given far too much play, these days.*

*– I think you're talking nonsense, says the black man.
It is true that he looks paler. Perhaps that is the moonlight
too, thinks Karl.*

– Probably, agrees Karl.

– Imagination can allow man to become anything he wants to be. It gives us everything that is human.

– And it creates the fears, the bogeymen, the devils which destroy us. Unreasoning terror. What other beast has fears like ours?

The black man gives him an intense glare. For a moment his eyes seem to shine with a feral gleam. But perhaps that is the moonlight again.

Karl is seventeen. A dupe of the Duce. Escaped from Berlin and claiming Italian citizenship, he now finds himself drafted into the Army. You can't win in Europe these days. It's bad. There is pain . . .

There is heat.

– Are you afraid, then? asks Karl's friend.

–Of course. I'm guilty, fearful, unfulfilled . . .

– Forget your guilts and your fears and you will be fulfilled.

– And will I be human?

–What are you afraid of?

KARL WAS SEVENTEEN. His mother had gone. His father had gone. His uncle, an Italian citizen, adopted him in 1934. Almost immediately Karl had been conscripted into the Army. He had no work. He had been conscripted under his uncle's new name of Giombini, but they knew he was a Jew really.

He had guessed he would be going to Ethiopia when all the lads in the barracks had been issued with tropical kit. Almost everyone had been sure that it would be Ethiopia.

And now, after a considerable amount of sailing and marching, here he was, lying in the dust near a burning mud hut in a town called Adowa with the noise of bombs and artillery all around him and a primitive spear stuck in his stomach, his rifle stolen, his body full of pain and his head full of regrets. His comrades ran about all round him, shooting at people he couldn't see. He didn't bother to call out. He would be punished for losing his rifle to a skinny brown man wearing a white sheet. He hadn't even had a chance to kill somebody.

He regretted first that he had left Berlin. Things might

have quietened down there eventually, after all. He had left only because of his parents' panic after the shop had been smashed. In Rome, he had never been able to get used to the food. He remembered the Berlin restaurants and wished he had had a chance to eat one good meal before going. He regretted, too, that he had not been able to realise his ambitions, once in the Army. A clever lad could rise rapidly to an important rank in wartime, he knew. A bomb fell nearby and the force of it stirred his body a little. Dust began to drift over everything. The yells and the shots and the sounds of the planes, the whine of the shells and the bombs, became distant. The dust made his throat itch and he used all his strength to stop himself from coughing and so make the pain from his wound worse. But he coughed at last and the spear quivered, a sharp black line against the dust which made everything else look so vague.

He watched the spear, forcing his eyes to focus on it. It was all he had.

You were supposed to forget about worldly ambitions when you were dying. But he felt cheated. He had got out of Berlin at the right time. Really, there was no point in believing otherwise. Friends of his would be in camps now, or deported to some frightful dungheap in North Africa. Italy had been a clever choice. Anti-Semitic feeling had never meant much in Italy. The fools who had gone to America and Britain might find themselves victims of pogroms at any minute. On the other hand the Scandinavian countries had seemed to offer an alternative. Perhaps he should have tried his luck in Sweden, where so many people spoke German and he wouldn't have felt too strange. A spasm of pain shook him. It felt as if his entrails were being stirred around by a big spoon. He had become so conscious of his innards. He could visualise them all – his lungs and his heart and his ruined stomach, the yards and yards of offal curled like so many pink, grey and yellow sausages inside him; then his cock, his balls, the muscles in his strong, naked legs; his fingers, his lips, his eyes, his nose and his ears. The black line faded. He forced it back into focus. His blood, no longer circulating smoothly through his veins and arteries, but pumping out of the openings around the blade of the spear, dribbling into the dust. Nothing would have happened in Germany after the first outbursts. It would have died down, the trouble. Hitler and his friends would have turned their attention to Russia, to the real enemies, the Communists. A funny little flutter started in his groin, below the spear blade. It was as if a moth were trying to get into the air, using his groin as a flying field, hopping about and beating its wings and failing to achieve takeoff. He tried to see, but fell back. He was thirsty. The line of the spear shaft had almost disappeared and he didn't bother to try to focus on it again.

The distant noises seemed to combine and establish close rhythms and counter-rhythms coupled with the beating of his heart. He recognised the tune. Some American popular song he had heard in a film. He had hummed the same song for six months after he had seen the film in Berlin. It must have been four years ago. Maybe longer. He wished that he had had a chance to make love to a woman. He had always disdained whores. A decent man didn't need whores. He wished that he had been to a whore and found out what it was like. One had offered last year as he walked to the railway station.

The film had been called *Sweet Music*, he remembered. He had never learned all the English words, but had made up words to sound like them.

> *There's a tavern in the town, in the town,*
> *When atroola setsen dahn, setsen dahn,*
> *Und der she sits on a luvaduvadee,*
> *Und never never sinka see.*
> *So fairdeewell mein on tooday . . .*

He had had ambitions to be an opera singer and he had had ambitions to be a great writer.

The potential had all been there, it was just a question of choosing. He might even have been a great general.

His possible incarnations marched before him through the dust.

And then he was dead.

– *You could be anything you wanted to be.* His friend kisses his shoulder.

– *Or nothing. Could I be a woman and give birth to five children?* Karl bites the black man.

The black man leaps up. He is a blurr. For a moment, in the half-light, Karl thinks that his friend is a woman and white and then an animal of some kind, teeth bared. The black man glowers at him – Don't do that to me!

And Karl wipes his lips.

He turns his back on his friend. Okay. You taste funny, anyway.

What Would You Do? (12)

You are a priest, devoutly religious, you are made miserable by the very idea of violence. You are, in every sense, a man of peace.

One morning you are cutting bread in the small hall attached to your church. You hear screams and oaths coming from the church itself. You hurry into the church, the knife still in your hand.

The soldier of the enemy currently occupying your country is in the act of raping a girl of about thirteen. He has beaten her and torn her clothes. He is just about to enter her. She whimpers. He grunts. You recognise the girl as a member of your parish. Doubtless she came to the church for your help. You shout, but the soldier pays no attention. You implore him to stop to no avail.

If you kill the soldier with your knife it will save the young girl from being hurt any further. It might even save her life. Nobody knows the soldier has entered the church. You could hide the body easily.

If you merely knock him out – even if that's possible – he will almost certainly take horrible reprisals on you, your church and its congregation. It has happened before, in other towns. Yet you want to save the girl.

What would you do?

13

At The Auschwitz Ball:
1944: Strings

The war in Europe has been won; but the air of Europe smells of blood. Nazis and Fascists have been defeated; but their leaders have not yet been destroyed. It is still touch-and-go even now, whether the surviving Nazis are to have another chance of power, or whether they can be made harmless for ever by their swift arraignment as war criminals. And make no mistake this is not simply a matter for self-evident criminals such as Goering, Rosenberg and those others guilty of outstanding crimes, or responsible for the orders which caused major atrocities.

I have before me about twenty dossiers from small, unimportant French villages, and some from better-known places. They are unemotional accounts based on the evidence of named witnesses, of events which occurred during the German occupation. The Massacre of Dun Les Plages on June 26, 1944; the destruction of the village of Manlay on July 31, 1944; the treatment and murder in the Gestapo barracks at Cannes – and so it goes on. Sometimes the names of the local Nazis responsible have been discovered and named; often not.

The full horror of these cold indictments are revealed by the photographs which accompany them. It is difficult to describe them. Two or three of the mildest only are reproduced here. The Nazis took delight in having themselves photographed with their victims while these were in their agony of outrage and torture. It is not a simple crime that is depicted, but a terrible degradation of man. All the most horrible instincts which survive in our subconscious, have come brutally out into the open. It is no relapse into savagery, because no savages ever behaved with such cold, unfeeling, educated brutality and shamelessness.

These dossiers are French. But the same story is repeated in every country the Germans occupied, and also from those countries which allied themselves with the Nazis. Arrests, deportations, questionings and punishment were all carried out with a deliberate maximum of brutality accompanied by every conceivable carnal licence. Like the concentration camps, these methods aimed at the destruction of confidence in democratic values; at inducing a total surrender to the Nazi terror.

They succeeded for a time – probably more than most people who have never lived under Nazi domination care to believe. That fear and horror of the Nazi bully has not yet been eradicated. The war will not be over until all the outraged millions of once-occupied Europe enjoy full confidence that democratic Governments can protect their rights, and that those who have offended are punished and broken. The Nazis mobilised the *Untermensch,* the sub-human, into their ranks. The wickedness he worked is a vivid memory, and it must be exorcised before Europe can have peace.

PICTURE POST, *June 23, 1945.*

– *Don't try that with me, you little white bastard! Karl displays his arms.*

– *I'm a black bastard now.*

– *We can soon change that.*

– *Oh, hell, I'm sorry, says Karl. – It was just an impulse.*

– *Well, says his friend grimly, you're certainly losing your inhibitions now, aren't you.*

Karl is eighteen. He is very lucky, along with the other members of the orchestra. His mother told him there was a point to learning, that you never knew when it came in useful, fiddle playing. And it was beautifully warm in the barracks. He hoped they would dance all night.

– Come back to bed, says Karl. – Please . . .

– I thought you were a nice, simple, uncomplicated sort of chap, says the black man. – That's what attracted me to you in the first place. Ah, well – it was my own fault, I suppose.

Karl is eighteen and playing Johann Strauss. How beautiful. How his mother would have loved it. There are tears in his eyes. He hoped they would dance forever! The Oswiecim Waltz!

– Well, I'm not at my best says Karl. – I wasn't when you met me. That's why I was in the Roof Garden.

– It's true, says his friend, that we hardly know each other yet.

KARL WAS EIGHTEEN. His mother had been given an injection some time ago and she had died. His father had probably been killed in Spain. Karl sat behind the screen with the other members of the orchestra and he played the violin.

That was his job in Auschwitz. It was the plum job and he had been lucky to get it. Others were doing much less pleasant work and it was so cold outside. The big barrack hall was well-heated for the Christmas Dance and all the guards and non-commissioned officers, their sweethearts and wives, were enjoying themselves thoroughly, in spite of rations being so short.

Karl could see them through a gap in the screen as he and the others played *The Blue Danube* for the umpteenth time that evening. Round and round went the brown and grey uniforms; round and round went the skirts and the dresses. Boots stamped on the uncarpeted boards of the hall. Beer flowed. Everyone laughed and joked and sang and enjoyed themselves. And behind the leather upholstered screen borrowed for the occasion the band played on.

Karl had two pullovers and a pair of thick corduroy trousers, but he hardly needed the second pullover, it was so warm. He was much better off than when he had first come to the camp with his mother. Not that he had actually

133

seen his mother at the camp, because they had been segregated earlier on. It had been awful at first, seeing the faces of the older inmates, feeling that you were bound to become like them, losing all dignity. He had suffered the humiliation while he summed up the angles and, while a rather poor violinist, had registered himself as a professional. It had done the trick. He had lost a lot of weight, of course, which was only to be expected. Nobody, after all, was doing very well, this winter. But he had kept his dignity and his life and there was no reason why he shouldn't go on for a long while as he was. The guards liked his playing. They were not very hot on Bach and Mozart and luckily neither was he. He had always preferred the lighter gayer melodies.

He shut his eyes, smiling as he enjoyed his own playing.

When he opened his eyes, the others were not smiling. They were all looking at him. He shut his eyes again.

– *Would you say you were a winner? asks Karl's friend.*

– *No. Everything considered, I'd say I was a loser. Aren't we all?*

– *Are we? With the proper encouragement you could be a winner. With my encouragement.*

– *Oh, I don't know. I'm something of a depressive, as you may have noticed.*

– *That's my point. You've never had the encouragement. I love you, Karl.*

– *For myself?*

– *Of course. I have a lot of influence. I could get your work sold for good prices. You could be rich.*

– *I suppose I'd like that.*

– *If I got you a lot of money, what would you do?*

– *I don't know. Give it back to you?*

– *I don't mean my money. I mean if your work sold well.*

– *I'd buy a yacht, I think. Go round the world. It's something I've always wanted to do. I went to Paris when I was younger.*

– *Did you like it?*

– *It wasn't bad.*

What Would You Do? (13)

You own a dog. It is a dog you inherited from a friend some years ago. The friend asked you to look after it for a short while and never returned.

Now the dog is getting old. You have never cared much for it, but you feel sympathetic towards it. It has become long in the tooth, it makes peculiar retching noises, it has difficulty eating and sometimes its legs are so stiff you have to carry it up and down stairs.

The dog is rather cur-like in its general demeanor. It has never had what you would call a noble character. It is nervous, cowardly and given to hysterical barking.

Because of the stiffness in its legs you take it to the veterinary clinic.

The dog has lived several years beyond its expected lifespan. Its eyes are failing and it is rather deaf.

You have the opportunity to ask the veterinary to destroy the dog. And yet the dog is in no pain or any particular discomfort most of the time. The vet says that it will go on quite happily for another year or so. You hate the idea of witnessing the dog's last agonies when its time does come to die. You have only a faint degree of affection for it. It would really be better if the vet got it over with now.

What would you say to the vet?

14

The Road to Tel-Aviv:
1947: Traps

ATIYAH: I have three comments to make. First, concerning what Reid said about Palestine having belonged to the Turks. Under Turkish suzerainty the Arabs were not a subject people, but partners with the Turks in the empire. Second, on what I considered was the false analogy – when Crossman said the Jews were unlucky in that they were, as he put it, the last comers into the fields of overseas settlement. He mentioned Australia. I would point out that the Arabs in Palestine do not belong to the same category as the aborigines of Australia. They belong to what was once a highly-civilised community, and before what you call overseas settlement in Palestine by the Jews was begun, the Arabs were re-awakening into a tremendous intellectual and spiritual activity after a period of decadence, so there can be no comparison between the two cases.

CROSSMAN: Tom, what do you think were the real mistakes of British policy which led up to what we all agree is an intolerable situation?

REID: The British Government during the first World War had induced the Arabs, who were in revolt against the Turks, to come in and fight on the Allied side. We made them a promise in the McMahon Declaration and then, without their knowledge, invited the Jews to come in and establish a national home. That was unwise and wicked. As I

understand it, the idea of the British Government
was that the Jews should come in and gradually become a majority. That was a secret understanding
and was doubly wicked.

PICTURE POST
Palestine: Can deadlock be broken?
Discussion between Edward Atiyah,
Arab Office; Thomas Reid, M.P.,
R.H.S. Crossman, M.P, and Prof.
Martin Buber, Prof. Sociology,
Jerusalem University, July 12, 1947.

– What does money mean to you, Karl?

– Well, security, I suppose, first and foremost.

*– You mean it can buy you security. A house, food, the
obvious comforts, power over others.*

*– I'm not sure about power over others. What has that
to do with security?*

– Oh it must have something to do with it.

*At nineteen, Karl is bent on vengeance and the regaining
of his rights. He has a .303 Lee Enfield rifle, some hand
grenades, a bayonet and a long dagger. He wears a khaki
shirt and blue jeans. On his head is a burnoose. He stands
on the bank overlooking the winding road to Tel-Aviv.
He lifts his head proudly into the sun.*

*– You can keep yourself to yourself, says Karl with a
grin. – Can't you.*

*– As long as others do. The dweller in the suburbs, Karl,
must pursue a policy of armed neutrality.*

*– I was brought up in the suburbs. I never saw it like
that. I don't know what things are like in Nigeria, mind
you . . .*

*At nineteen, Karl has a girl whom he has left behind in
Joppa. There are five friends with him on the road. He sees
a dust-cloud approaching. It must be the jeep. With the
veil of his burnoose, Karl covers his mouth against the
dust.*

– Much the same, says Karl's friend. – Much the same.

KARL WAS NINETEEN. His mother had been gassed, his father had been gassed. At least, that was as far as he knew. He had been lucky. In 1942 he and his uncle had managed to sneak into Palestine and had not been caught as illegal immigrants. But Karl had soon realised the injustice of British rule and now he belonged to the Irgun Tsva'i Leumi, pledged to drive the British out of Palestine if they had to kill every single British man, woman or child to do it. It was time the Jews turned. There would never be another pogrom against the Jews that was not answered in kind. It was the only way.

He squinted against the glare of the sun, breathing with some difficulty through the gauze of his headdress. The air was dry dusty and stale. There was no doubt about the single jeep droning along the road from Abid to Tel-Aviv. It was British. He gestured down to his friend David. David, too, was masked. David, too, had a Lee Enfield rifle. He handed up the field-glasses to Karl. Karl took them, adjusted them, saw that there were two soldiers in the jeep – a sergeant and a corporal. They would do.

Further along the road, in the shade of a clump of stunted palms, waited the rest of the section. Karl signalled to them. He swept the surrounding hills with his glasses to check that there was no one about. Even a goatherd could prove an embarrassment, particularly if he were an Arab. The parched hills were deserted.

You could hear the jeep quite clearly now, its engine whining as it changed gear and took an incline.

Karl unclipped a grenade from his belt.

The others left the shade of the palms and got into the ditch behind the bank, lying flat, their rifles ready. Karl looked at David. The boy's dark eyes were troubled. Karl signalled for David to join him. He pulled the pin from the grenade. David imitated him, unclipping a grenade, pulling out the pin, holding down the safety.

Karl felt his legs begin to tremble. He felt ill. The heat was getting to him. The jeep was almost level. He sprang up, steadied himself on the top of the bank, and threw the grenade in a gentle, graceful curve. It was a beautiful throw. It went straight into the back seat of the jeep. The soldiers looked astonished. They glanced back. They glanced at Karl. The jeep's pace didn't slacken. It blew up.

There was really no need for the second grenade which David threw and which landed in the road behind the remains of the jeep.

The two soldiers had been thrown out of the wreckage. They were both alive, though broken and bleeding. One of them was trying to draw his side-arm. Karl walked slowly towards him, his .303 cocked. With a casual movement of his foot he kicked the pistol from the sergeant's hand as the man tried to get the hammer back. The sergeant's face was covered in blood. Out of the mess stared two blue eyes. The ruined lips moved, but there were no words. Nearby, the corporal sat up.

The rest of the group joined Karl.

"I'm glad you weren't killed," Karl said in his guttural English.

"Aaah!" said the corporal. "You dirty Arab bastards." He hugged his broken right arm.

"We are Jews," said David, ripping his mask down.

"I don't believe it," said the corporal.

"We are going to hang you," said Karl, pointing at the palms, visible beyond the bank.

David went to look at the jeep. The whole back section was buckled and one of the wheels was off. Some piece of machinery still gasped under the bonnet. David reached into the jeep and turned the engine off. There was a smell of leaking petrol. "It's not much use to us," said David.

"What do you bloody mean?" said the corporal in horror. "What the fuck do you bloody mean?"

"It's a message," said Karl, "from us to you."

– I've made up my mind, says Karl's friend as he busily massages Karl's buttocks. – I'm going to take you with me when I go home. You'll like it. It isn't everyone I meet I'd do that for.

Karl makes no reply. He is feeling rather detached. He doesn't remember when he felt so relaxed.

What Would You Do? (14)

You are very attracted to a girl of about seventeen who is the daughter of one of your parent's friends. The girl lives with her parents in the country. You take every opportunity to see her (you are not much older than her, yourself) but although you take her out to formal parties a couple of times and to the cinema once, you can't be sure how she feels towards you. The more you see of her the more you want to make love to her. But you realise she is quite young and you don't want to see yourself in the role of the seducer. You would feel perfectly happy about it if she made the first move. But she is shy. She plainly likes you. Probably she is waiting for you to make the first move. You are passing through the part of the world where she and her parents live and you decide to visit the house and ask if you can stay the night, as it's quite late. You rather hope that, at last, you will be able to find an opportunity to make love to the girl.

You arrive at the house. The door is opened by the girl's mother, an attractive woman in her early forties. She is very welcoming. You tell her your story and she says that of course you can stay, for as long as you like. She regrets that you will not be able to see her husband because he is away for some days on a business trip. Her daughter is out – "with one of her boyfriends." You feel disappointed.

You have dinner with the mother and you and she drink quite a lot of wine. The mother makes no doubt about the fact that she finds you attractive. After dinner sitting together on a couch, you find that you are holding hands with her.

You have a mixture of feelings. She is attractive and you do feel that you want to make love, but you are rather afraid of her experience. Secondly, you feel that if you sleep with her, it will complicate the situation so much that you will never have an opportunity to make love to her daughter, whom you feel you could easily fall in love with. You also need the mother's good will.

Would you get up from the couch and make an excuse in order to go to bed. Would you make love to the mother up to a point and then claim that you were too drunk to go further. Would you pretend to be ill? Would you give in completely to your desires of the moment and sleep with the mother, in spite of the inevitable situation which this would lead to? Would you hope that the daughter would be so intrigued by your having slept with her mother that she would make it clear that she, too, wanted to sleep with you (you have heard that such things happen)? Or would you feel that the whole problem was too much, leave the house and resolve never to see any member of the family ever again?

15

Big Bang in Budapest: 1956: Leaving Home

In the Troodos hills in the west of Cyprus, the job is being carried out by Number 45 Commando of the Royal Marines, together with two companies of the Gordon Highlanders. The Commando arrived in Cyprus last September; its headquarters are now in Platres, near Troodos. Its commanding officer, Lt.-Col. N. H. Tailyour, DSO, recalled its record to date. "In early November we took the first haul of EOKA arms. We shot and captured the brother of the Bishop of Kyrenia (who was deported with the Archbishop) while he was trying to break through a cordon with some important documents ... So far we have killed two men ... We have been ambushed seven times, and lost one marine killed and seven wounded." A lot more has happened since then.

PICTURE POST, *April 7, 1956.*

"My daughter was one of the ten people who went into the Radio building. They were asked to wait on the balcony while the business was discussed. The students below thought they had been pushed out. They tried to crush through the door and the police opened fire. I did not see my daughter fall down. They said she fell and the security police carried her away. She may not be dead. Perhaps it were better she were."

PICTURE POST, *Hungarian woman, November 5, 1956,*

Picture Post brings you this week the most dramatic exclusive of the war in Egypt – the first documentary record of life behind the Egyptian lines after the invasion of Port Said. How this story was obtained by correspondent William Richardson and photographer Max Scheler is in itself one of the remarkable stories of the campaign. While the fires at Port Said still burned, Richardson was at the British front line at El Cäp watching the Egyptians dig in 1,000 yards south. Three weeks later he stood at those same Egyptian positions watching the British across the lines and getting a briefing on the campaign from Brigadier Anin Helmini, one of Nasser's most brilliant young generals. Yet to negotiate that 1,000 yards between the British and Egyptian lines Richardson had to travel some 5,600 times that distance, flying from Port Said to Cyprus and from there to Athens and Rome. There the Egyptian Embassy granted him a visa after he told them he had been in Port Said and wanted to see both sides. In a month, he was accredited to three forces – British, Egyptian and United Nations, a total of 12 nationalities in uniform.

PICTURE POST, *December 17, 1956.*

– Is your only pleasure making me feel pleasure? Karl asks.

– Of course not.

–Well, you don't seem to be getting any fun out of this. Not physical, anyway.

– Cerebral pleasures can be just as nice. It depends what turns you on, surely?

Karl turns over. – There's something pretty repressed about you, he says. – Something almost dead.

–You know how to be offensive don't you? A short time ago you were just an ordinary London lad. Now you're behaving like the bitchiest little pansy I ever saw.

– Maybe I like the role.

Karl is twenty. He scents escape at last. He has survived through the War, through the Communist take-over. Now

*there is a way out. He prays that nothing will happen to
frustrate his plans this time . . .*

*– And maybe I don't. When I said you could have any-
thing you wanted I didn't mean a bra and suspender belt.
The black man turns away in disgust.*

*– You said anything was worth trying, didn't you? I think
I'd look rather nifty. A few hormone jabs, a pump or two
of silicone in my chest. I'd be a luscious, tropical beauty.
Wouldn't you love me more?*

*Karl is twenty. His brain is sharp. He tears up his party
membership card. Time for a change.*

*– Stop that! orders Karl's friend. – Or I won't bother.
You can leave now.*

– Who's being narrow minded, then!

KARL IS TWENTY. Both his mother and his father had been
killed in the pre-war pogroms. He had survived in Buda-
pest by changing his name and keeping undercover until
the war was over. When the new government was installed,
he became a member of the Communist party, but he didn't
tell his friends. That would have been pointless, since part
of his work involved making discreet enquiries for the Russian controlled security department on the Westbahnhof.

Now he was working out his best route to the Austrian
border. He had joined with his fellow students in the least
aggressive of the demonstrations against the Russians and
had established himself as a patriot. When the Russians
won – as they must win – he would be in Vienna on his
way to America. Other Hungarians would vouch for him
– a victim, like themselves, of Russian imperialism.

Earlier that day he had contacted the hotel where the
tourists were staying. They told him that there were some
cars due to leave for Austria in the afternoon by the big
suspension bridge near the hotel. He had described himself
as a "known patriot" whom the secret police were even
now hunting down. They had been sympathetic and assured
him of their help.

Lenin Street was comparatively quiet after the fighting
which, yesterday, had blasted it, into ruins. He picked his

way through the rubble, ducking behind a fallen tree as a Russian tank appeared, its treads squeaking protest as they struck obstacle after obstacle.

Karl reached the riverside. A few people came running up the boulevard but there didn't seem to be anyone behind them. Karl decided it was safe to continue. He could see the bridge from here. Not far to go.

There came the sudden slamming cacophony of automatic cannon a few blocks to the east; a howl from a hundred throats at least; the decisive rattle of machine guns; the sound of running feet. From out of a street opposite him Karl saw about fifty freedom fighters, most of them armed with rifles and a few with tommy-guns, dash like flushed rats onto the boulevard, glance around and then run towards the bridge. He cursed them. Why couldn't they have fled in the other direction?

But he decided to follow them, at a distance.

On the suspension bridge he saw some tanks. He hoped they had been immobilised. Bodies were being thrown over the side into the Danube. He hoped they were Russian bodies. He began to look for the cars. A new Citroen, green, one of the tourists had told him, and a Volkswagen. He peered through the gaps in the ranks of the running men. He began to run himself.

And then the automatic cannon started once more. This time it was directly ahead and it was joined by the guns of the tanks. The freedom fighters fell down. Some got up and crawled into doorways, firing back. Karl fell flat, rolling to the railings and looking to see if there was a way down to the river. He might be able to swim the rest of the distance. He looked across the Danube. He could still make it. He would survive.

Tanks came towards him, he made a vain attempt to get through the railings and then lay still, hoping they would think him dead.

More rifle and tommy-gun fire. More Russian gunfire. A shout. A strangled scream.

Karl opened his eyes. One of the tanks was on fire, its camouflaged sides scorched, its red star smeared with blood.

The tank's driver had tried to get out of his turret and had been shot to pieces. The other tanks rumbled on. The fighting became more distant. Karl glanced at his watch. No more than five minutes before the cars left.

He got cautiously to his feet.

A Russian's head appeared in the turret behind the corpse of the driver. The man's flat features were tormented. He was doubtless badly wounded. He saw Karl. Karl put up his hands to show that he was unarmed. He smiled an ingratiating smile. The Russian aimed a pistol at him. Karl tried to think what to do.

He felt the impact as the bullet struck his skull. He went back against the railings and collapsed without seeing the Danube again.

– You seem to think I'm trying to corrupt your morals or something. You've got hold of the wrong end of the stick. I was simply talking about expanding your range of choices. I don't know what to make of you Karl.

– Then we're even.

– I might have to change my mind about you. I'm sorry, but that's the way it is. If I'm to adopt you, it will be on very strict terms. I don't want you to embarrass me.

– That goes for me, too.

– Now don't be insolent, Karl.

What Would You Do? (15)

You live in a poor country, though you yourself are comparatively rich.

There is a famine in the country and many of the people are starving. You want to help them. You can afford to give the local people in the village about fifty pounds. But the number of people in the village is at least two hundred. If each receives part of the money you have, it will buy them enough to live on for perhaps another four days.

Would you give them the money on condition it was spent on the people most in need? Or on condition that it was spent on the children? Or would you select a handful of people you thought deserved the money most? Or would you hand it over to them and ask them to divide as they saw fit?

16

Camping In Kenya: 1959: Smoke

Here is the grim record as far as it can be added up in figures: more than a thousand Africans hanged for serious crimes, 9,252 Mau Mau convicts jailed for serious offences, and 44,000 "detainees", guilty of lesser Mau Mau offences, in rehabilitation prison camps. In these camps, in carefully graded groups, Mau Mau adherents are re-educated as decent citizens ... To make return possible mental attitudes have to be changed ... Perhaps "soul-washing" is not too strong a word for an organised process aimed at teaching civilised behaviour and the duties, as well as the rights, of citizenship ...

Soldiers and police have won the long battle of the bush against ill-armed men fighting for what they believe to be a good cause. All but the broken remnants, under their broken leader Dedan Kimathi, have been killed or rounded up. The battle to turn Mau Mau adherents into decent citizens goes well.

But the battle to remove the underlying causes, social and economic, of the anti-white hate that created Mau Mau, will go on for long years. There, too, a hopeful beginning has been made. Princess Margaret's visit marks not just the end of a long nightmare, but the beginning of a new era of multiracial integration – and of fairer shares for the African – in lovely Kenya.

If the Malayan and Korean campaigns had drawn most attention during the early part of the 1950s, the British Army had had much to do elsewhere. In Kenya the Mau Mau gangs, recruited from the Kikuyu tribe, had taken to the dense rain forests from which they made sorties to attack Europeans and Africans. The Kikuyu were land hungry. Their discontent was used to further the aspirations of urban Africans for political independence. Over eight years, 1952–60, British battalions, batteries and engineer squadrons, supported by small but intensely-worked communications and administrative teams, broke the movement in alliance with a devoted police and civil government organisation, many of them Africans or Asian settlers. Only when this had been done was the cause of Kenyan independence advanced.

HISTORY OF THE BRITISH ARMY
Ed. Brigadier Peter Young and Lt.-Col. J. P. Lawford.
Ch. 32 AFTER THE WAR, *by Brig. Anthony H. Farrar-Hockley, DCO, MBE, MC.*
Arthur Barker, 1970

– *You're right. There's no such thing as innocence, says Karl.*

– *Absolutely. It's as abstract as "justice" and "virtue" – or, for that matter, "morality".*

– *Right. There's certainly no justice!*

– *And far too much morality!*

They laugh.

– *I didn't realise you had blue eyes, says Karl, astonished.*

– *They're only blue in some lights. Look, I'll turn my head. See?*

– *They're still blue.*

– *What about this? Green? Brown?*

– *Blue.*

Karl has reached his majority. He's twenty one. Signed on for another seven years' stint in the Mob. There's no life like it!

149

– You're just telling me that, says his friend anxiously.
How about now?

*– Well, I suppose you could say they looked a bit green-
ish,* says Karl kindly.

*– It's envy, old chap, at your lovely big bovine brown
ones.*

– Give us a kiss.

Twenty one and the world his oyster. Cyprus, Aden
Singapore. Wherever the British Army's needed. Karl is a
sergeant already. And he could do the officer exam soon.
He's used to commanding, by now. Twice decorated? No
sweat!

– Where?

– Don't make me laugh.

KARL WAS TWENTY-ONE. His mother was forty five. His
father was forty seven. They lived in Hendon, Middlesex,
in a semi-detached house which Karl's father, who had
never been out of work in his life, had begun to buy just
before the war. His father had been doing indispensable
war work and so had not had to serve in the Army (he was
a boiler engineer). His father had thoughtfully changed his
name to Gower in 1939, partly because it sounded too German, partly because, you never knew, if the Germans won,
it sounded too Jewish. Not, of course, that it was a Jewish
name. Karl's dad denied any such suggestion vehemently.
It was an old Austrian name, resembling a name attached
to one of the most ancient noble houses in Vienna. That's
what Karl's grandfather had said, anyway. Karl had been
called after his grandad. Karl's father's name was English
– Arnold.

Karl had been in the Army since he had joined up as a
boy-entrant in 1954. He had seen a lot of service since then.
But for the past two years he'd been out in Kenya, clearing
up the Mau Mau business, which seemed to drag on forever. Off duty, it was a smashing life. The worst of the ter-
rorism was over and it wasn't nearly so dangerous as it had
been. Karl had an Indian girl-friend in Nairobi and he got
there as often as he could to fuck the shit out of her. She was

a hot little bitch though he had a sneaking suspicion she'd given him his last dose of crabs. You could never tell with crabs, mind you, so he gave her the benefit of the doubt. What a muff! What tits! It gave you a hard on just thinking about them. Lovely!

The jeep pulled up at the gates of the compound. Another day's work was beginning. Karl was part of the special Intelligence team working closely with the Kenya Police in this area, where there was still a bit of Mau Mau mischief. Privately, Karl thought it would go on forever. They didn't have a hope in hell of governing themselves. He looked at the inmates behind the barbed wire. It made you smile to think about it. Offering it, that was different, if you had to keep them under control. Of course you can have independence – in two million bloody years! Ho, ho, ho!

He scratched his crotch with his swagger stick and grinned to himself as his driver presented their pass. The jeep bumped its way over the uneven mud track into the compound.

The Kikuyu prisoners stood, or sat, or leaned around, looking with dull eyes at the jeep as it pulled up outside the main Intelligence hut. Some distance away, squatting on the ground, were about a hundred natives listening to Colonel Wibberley giving them their usual brainwashing (or what would be a brainwashing if they had any brains to wash, thought Karl. He knew bloody well that you released the buggers as decontaminated only to get half of them back sooner or later with blood on their bloody hands). Oh, what a horrible lot they were, in their reach-me-down flannel shorts, their tattered shirts, their old tweed jackets, their bare scabby feet, some of them with silly grins all over their ugly mugs. He saluted Private Peterson who was on guard outside the hut as usual. He already felt like an officer.

"Morning, sarge," said Peterson as he passed. Bastard!

Corporal Anderson, all red and sweaty as usual, was on duty at the desk when Karl entered. Anderson always looked as if he'd just been caught in the act of pulling his plonker – shifty, seedy.

"You are an unwholesome little sod, Corporal Anderson," said Karl by way of greeting. Corporal Anderson tittered. "What's new, then? Blimey, couldn't you get a stronger bulb, I can't see for looking."

"I'll put a chit in, sarge."

"And hurry up about it. Is old Lailu ready to talk yet?"

"I haven't been in there this morning, sarge. The lieutenant . . ."

"What about the bleeding lieutenant?"

"He's away, sarge. That's all."

"Bloody good fucking thing, too, little shit-faced prick, little upper-class turd," mumbled Karl to himself as he went through the papers on his desk. Same problem as yesterday. Find out what Lailu knew about the attack on the Kuanda farm a week ago. Lailu had been in the raid, all right, because he'd been recognised. And he'd used to work at the farm. He claimed to have been in his own village, but that was a lie. Who could prove it? And he'd been in the camp more than once. He was a known Mau Mau. And he was a killer. Or knew who the killers were, which was the same thing.

"I'll have a word with him, I think," said Karl, sipping the tea the corporal brought him. "I'll have to get unpleasant today if he don't open his fucking mouth. And I'll have him all to my fucking self, won't I, corp?"

"Yes, sarge," said Corp, his thick lips writhing, his hot, shifty eyes seething, as if Karl had caught him out at some really nasty form of self-abuse.

"Ugh, you are horrible" said Karl, automatically.

"Yes, sarge."

Karl snorted with laughter. "Go and tell them to take our little black brother into the special room, will you?"

"Yes, sarge." Corporal Anderson went through the door into the back of the hut. Karl heard him talking to the guards. A bit later Anderson came back.

"He's ready, sarge."

"Thank you, corporal," said Karl in his crisp, decisive voice. He put his cigarettes and matches in the top pocket of his shirt, picked up his swagger stick and crossed the

152

mud floor to the inner door. "Oh," he said, hesitating before entering, "if our good lieutenant should come calling, let me know would you, corporal?"

"Yes, sarge. I get you."

"And don't pick your nose while I'm gone, will you, corporal?"

"No, sarge."

Karl thought about that little Indian bint in Nairobi. He'd give a lot to be taking her knickers down at this moment, of getting her legs open and fucking the arse off of her. But duty called.

He whistled as he walked along the short, dark passage to the special room. It was bleeding hot in here, worse than a bloody native hut. It stank of fucking Kikuyu.

He gave the guard at the door of the special room his officer's salute, with the swagger stick touching the peak of his well-set cap.

He went into the special room and turned on the light.

Lailu sat on the bench, his bony knees sticking up at a peculiar angle, his eyes wide and white. There was a lot of sweat in his thin moustache.

"Hello, Mr. Lailu," said Karl with his cold grin, "how are you feeling this fine summer morning? A bit warm? Sorry we can't open a window for you, but you can see for yourself, there isn't one. That's probably against fire regulations. You could complain about that. Do you want to complain to me, Mr. Lailu?"

Lailu shook his black head.

"Because you've got your rights, you know. Lots and lots of rights. You've heard the lectures? Yes, of course you have, more than once, because you've been here more than once, haven't you, Mr. Lailu?"

Lailu made no response at all to this. Karl went up to him and stood very close, looking down on him. Lailu didn't look back. Karl grabbed the man's ear and twisted it so that Lailu's lips came together tightly. "Because I remember my trade-mark, you see, Mr. Lailu. That little scar, that's not a tribal scar, is it, Mr. Lailu? That little scar isn't a Mau Mau scar, is it? That is a Sergeant Gower scar, eh?"

"Yes, boss," said Lailu. "Yes, boss."

"Good."

Karl stepped back and leaned against the door of the special room. "We're going to keep everything informal, Mr. Lailu. You know your rights, don't you?"

"Yes, boss."

"Good."

Karl grinned down on Lailu again. "You were at the Kuanda farm last week, weren't you?"

"No, boss."

"Yes you were!" Karl began to breathe quickly, the swagger stick held firmly in his two hands. "Weren't you?"

"No, boss. Lailu not Mau Mau, boss. Lailu good boy, boss."

"Yes, a good little liar." The swagger stick left Karl's right hand almost without him thinking about it. It struck Lailu on the top of his head. Lailu whimpered. "Now I won't do that again, Lailu, because that's not the way I work, is it?"

"Don't know, boss."

"Is it?"

"No, boss."

"Good." Karl took out his packet of Players and selected one. He put the cigarette between his lips and he put the packet carefully back into his pocket. He took out his matches and he lit the cigarette so that it was burning just right. He put the matches back in his pocket and neatly he buttoned the pocket. He drew a deep puff on the cigarette. "Smoke, Lailu?"

Lailu trembled all over. "No, boss. Please."

"Shit, Lailu? You look as if you feel like one. Use the pot over there. Get them manky pants down, Lailu."

"Please, boss."

Karl moved quickly. It was always best to move quickly. He grabbed the top of the Kikuyu's shorts and ripped them down to his knees, exposing the shrivelled, scarred genitals.

"Oh, I have been here before, haven't I, Lailu?"

154

– That's better, says Karl.

– You're insatiable, says his friend admiringly. I've got to admit it, for all your faults.

– What's the time? Karl asks. – My watch has stopped.

– It must be coming up for morning, says his friend.

What Would You Do? (16) *

You and your sister have been captured by your enemies. They are brutal enemies.

They want information from you concerning your friends. They say they will make you responsible for your sister's safety. If you tell them all they wish to know she will go free. If you do not they will humiliate, terrorise and torture her in every way they know.

You are aware that should they catch your friends they will do the same thing to at least some of them, perhaps all of them.

Whom will you betray?

17

So Long Son Lon:
1968: Babies

Quite apart from the enormous present importance
of South Vietnam and our actions there, I have often
reflected – as one who was tempted to become a professional historian – that the story of Vietnam, of
South-East Asia, and of American policy there forms
an extraordinarily broad case history involving almost all the major problems that have affected the
world as a whole in the past 25 years. For the strands
of the Vietnam history include the characteristics
of French colonial control compared to colonial control elsewhere, the end of the colonial period, the
inter-relation and competition of nationalism and
Communism, our relation to the Soviet Union and
Communist China and their relationships with each
other, our relation to the European colonial power –
France – and at least since 1954 – the relation of Vietnam to the wider question of national independence
and self-determination in South-East Asia and indeed throughout Asia ...

... So all over South-East Asia there is today a
sense of confidence – to which Drew Middleton
again testified from his trip. Time has been bought,
and used. But that confidence is not solid or secure
for the future. It would surely be disrupted if we
were, in President Johnson's words, to permit a
Communist takeover in South Vietnam either
through withdrawal or "under the cloak of a mean-
ingless agreement". If, on the contrary, we proceed

on our present course – with measured military actions and with every possible non-military measure, and searching always for an avenue to peace – the prospects for a peaceful and secure South-East Asia now appear brighter than they have been at any time since the nations of the area were established on an independent basis.

THE PATH TO VIETNAM, *by William P. Bundy.*
An address given before the National Student
Association convention held at the
University of Maryland, August 15, 1967
United States Information Service, American
Embassy, London, August 1967

"We were all psyched up, and as a result when we got there the shooting started, almost as a chain reaction. The majority of us had expected to meet VC combat troops, but this did not turn out to be so . . . After they got in the village, I guess you could say that the men were out of control."

G.I. Dennis. Conti.

"They just kept walking towards us . . . You could hear the little girl saying, 'No, no . . .' All of a sudden, the GIs opened up and cut them down."

Ron Haeberle, reporter.

"It's just that they didn't know what they were supposed to do; killing them seemed like a good idea, so they did it. The old lady who fought so hard was probably a VC. Maybe it was just her daughter."

Jay Roberts, reporter.

MY LAI *4:* A REPORT ON THE MASSACRE AND ITS
    AFTERMATH.
Seymour M. Hersh, Harper's Magazine May 1970.

Mr. Daniel Ellsberg will surrender tomorrow in Boston where he lives. He was charged on Friday with being unlawfully in possession of secret documents, and a warrant was issued for his arrest. Since

he was named on June 16, by a former reporter of
the 'New York Times', as the man who provided
the paper with its copy of a Pentagon report, Mr.
Ellsberg and his wife have been in hiding. The Pentagon is about to hand over its Vietnam study to
Congress for confidential perusal. On Saturday the
Justice Department sought to convince the Court
that indiscriminate publication of further documents
from the study would endanger troops in South Vietnam and prejudice the procedures for obtaining the
release of prisoners.

THE GUARDIANS, *June 28, 1971.*

*– You're not slow, are you? says Karl's friend. – And to
think I was worried. Now I think I'll get some sleep.*

– Not yet, says Karl.

– Yes, now. I'm not feeling too well, as it happens.

*– You are looking a bit grey. Karl inspects the black
man's flesh. Compared with his own skin, it is quite pale.*

Karl is twenty-two and it's his last few months in the
Army. The past five months have been spent in Vietnam.
Although he's seen only one VC in that time, he's tired and
tense and fearful. He jokes a lot, like his buddies. There is
heat, sticky sweat, jungle, mud, flies, poverty, death, but no
Viet Cong. And this is a place reputedly thick with them.

*– I'll be all right when I've rested, says Karl's friend.
You've worn me out, that's all.*

Karl reaches out the index finger of his right hand and
traces his nail over his friend's lips. *– You can't be that
tired.*

Twenty-two and weary. A diet of little more than cold
C-rations for weeks at a stretch. No change of clothing.
Crashing around in the jungle. For nothing, It wasn't like
the John Wayne movies. Or maybe it was. The shit and the
heat – and then the action coming fast and hard. The vic-
tory. The tough captain proving he was right to drive the
men so hard, after all. The bowed heads as they honoured

158

*dead buddies. Not many could stop the tears ... But so
far all they had was the shit and the heat.*

*Karl's friend opens his lips. Karl hasn't noticed before
that his friend's teeth are rather stained.*

– Just let me rest a little.

KARL WAS TWENTY-TWO. His mother was forty-five. His
father was forty-four. His father managed a hardware store
in Phoenix, Arizona. His mother was a housewife.

Karl was on a big mission at last. He felt that if he survived the mission then it would all be over and he could
look forward to going home, back to his job as his father's
assistant. It was all he wanted.

He sat shoulder to shoulder with his buddies in the shivering chopper as it flew them to the combat area. He tried
to read the tattered *X-Men* comic book he had brought
along, but it was hard to concentrate. Nobody, among the
other members of his platoon, was talking much.

Karl's hands were sweating and there was dark grease on
them from the helicopter, from his rifle. The grease left his
fingertips on the pages of the comic book. He tucked the
book into his shirt and buttoned his shirt. He smoked a
joint handed to him by Bill Leinster who, like two thirds
of the platoon, was black. The joint didn't do anything for
him. He shifted the extra belt of M16 ammo to a more comfortable position round his neck. He was overloaded with
equipment. It would almost worth a battle to get rid of
some of the weight of cartridges he was carrying.

He wondered what would be happening in Son Lon now.
The hamlet had already been hit by the morning's artillery
barrage and the gunships had gone in ahead. The first platoon must have arrived already. Karl was in the second
platoon of four. Things would be warming up by the time
he landed.

The note of the chopper's engine changed and Karl
knew they were going down. He thought he heard gunfire.
He wiped the grease off his hands onto the legs of his pants.
He took a grip on his M16. Everyone else was beginning
to straighten up, ready themselves. None of the faces

showed much emotion and Karl hoped that his face looked the same.

"After what they did to Goldberg," said Bill Leinster in a masculine growl, "I'm going to get me a lot of ears."

Karl grinned at him.

The chopper's deck tilted a little as the machine settled. Sergeant Grossman got the door open. Now Karl could hear the firing quite clearly, but he could only see a few trees through the door. "Okay, let's go," said Sergeant Grossman grimly. He sprayed a few rounds into the near-by trees and jumped out. Karl was the fifth man to follow him. There were eight other helicopters on the ground, a patch of mud entirely surrounded by trees. Karl could see four big gunships firing at something ahead. Two more big black transports were landing. The noise of their rotors nearly drowned the noise of the guns. It seemed that the first platoon was still in the landing zone. Karl saw Sergeant Grossman run across to where Lieutenant Snider was standing with his men. They conferred for a few moments and then Grossman ran back. Snider's platoon moved off into the jungle. After waiting a moment or two Grossman ordered his men forward, entering the line of trees to the left and at an angle to where Snider's men had gone in. Karl assumed that the VC in this area had either been killed or had retreated back to the hamlet. There was no firing from the enemy as yet. But he kept himself alert. They could be anywhere in the jungle and they could attack in a dozen different ways. He suddenly got a craving for a Coors. Only a Coors in a giant-size schooner, the glass misted with frost. And a Kool, enjoyed in that downtown bar where his father's friends always drank on Saturday nights. That was what he'd have when he got home. The firing in front intensified. The first platoon must have met head on with the VC. Karl peered through the trees but could still see nothing. Sergeant Grossman waved at them to proceed with increased caution. The comic book was scratching his stomach. He regretted putting it in there. He glanced back at Bill Leinster. Leinster had the only grenade launcher in this team. Karl wondered if Leinster shouldn't be ahead of them, with the machine gunner and the sergeant. On the other hand, their rear might not be protected by the squad supposed to be flanking them and there was no cover on either side, as far as he knew, though technically there should have been. You could be hit from anywhere. He began to inspect the ground for mines, walking carefully in the footprints of the man in front of him. Sergeant Grossman paused and for a second they halted. Karl could now see a flash of red brick through the trees. They had reached the hamlet of Son Lon. There was a lot of groundfire.

Suddenly Karl was ready. He knew he would do well on this mission. His whole body was alert.

They moved into the hamlet.

The first thing they saw were VC bodies in black silk pyjamas and coolie hats. They were mostly middle-aged men and some women. There didn't seem to be too many weapons about. Maybe these had been collected up by the first platoon.

Two or three hootches were burning fitfully where they had been blasted by grenades and subsequently set on fire. A couple of the red brick houses bore evidence of having been in the battle. Outside one of them lay the bloody corpse of a kid of around eight or nine. That was the worst part, when they used kids to draw your fire, or even throw grenades at you. More firing came from the left, Karl turned, ducking and ready, his rifle raised, but no attack came. They proceeded warily into the village. Leinster, on command from Grossman, loaded his grenade launcher and started firing into the huts and houses as they passed, in case any VC should still be in there. It was menacingly safe, thought Karl, wondering what the VC were waiting for. Or maybe there hadn't been as many slopes in the hamlet as Captain Heffer had anticipated. Or maybe they were in the paddy-fields on the left and right of the village.

Karl really wanted to fire at something. Just one VC would do. It would justify everything else.

They entered the centre of the village, the plaza. Lieutenant Snider and his men were already there, rounding up civilians. There were a lot of bodies around the plaza,

161

mainly women and children. Karl was used to seeing corpses, but he had never seen so many. He was filled with disgust for the Vietnamese. They really had no human feelings. They were just like the Japs had been, and the Chinese in Korea. What was the point of fighting for them?

One of the kids in the group which had been rounded up ran forward. He held a coke bottle in his hand, offering it to the nearest soldier. The soldier was Henry Tabori. Karl knew him.

Tabori backed away from the boy and fired his M16 from the hip. The M16 was an automatic. The boy got all of it, staggering backwards and falling into the gang of villagers. Some of the women and old men started to shout. Some fell to their knees, wringing their hands. Karl had seen pictures of them doing that. Lieutenant Snider turned away with a shrug. Tabori put a new magazine into his rifle. By this time the other five men were firing into the ranks of the civilians. They poured scores of rounds into them. Blood appeared on the jerking bodies. Bits of chipped bone flew.

Karl saw Sergeant Grossman watching the slaughter. Grossman's face was thoughtful. Then Grossman said: "Okay, Leinster. Give it to 'em." He indicated the huts which had so far not been blasted. Leinster loaded his grenade launcher and began sending grenades through every doorway he could see. People started to run out. Grossman shot them down as they came. His machine-gunner opened up. One by one the other boys started firing. Karl dropped to a kneeling position, tucked his rifle hard against his shoulder, set the gun to automatic, and sent seventeen rounds into an old man as he stumbled from his hootch, his hands raised in front of his face, his legs streaming with blood. He put a fresh magazine into the rifle. The next time he fired he got a woman. The woman, with a dying action, rolled over onto a baby. The baby wasn't much good without its mother. Karl stepped closer and fired half his magazine into the baby. All the huts and houses were smoking, but people kept running out. Karl killed some more of them. Their numbers seemed to be endless.

Grossman shouted for them to cease firing, then led them at a run out of the plaza and along a dirt road. "Get 'em out of the huts," Grossman told his men. "Round the bastards up."

Karl and a negro called Keller went into one of the huts and kicked the family until they moved out into the street. There were two old men, an old woman, two young girls, a boy and a woman with a baby. Karl and Keller waved their rifles and made the family join the others in the street. They did not wait for Grossman's orders to fire.

Some of the women and the older girls and boys tried to put themselves between the soldiers and the smaller children. The soldiers continued to fire until they were sure they were all dead. Leinster began to giggle. Soon they were all giggling. They left the pile of corpses behind them and some of them swaggered as they walked. "We sure have got a lot of VC today," said Keller, wiping his forehead with a rag.

Karl looked back. He saw a figure rising from the pile of corpses. It was a girl of about thirteen, dressed in a black smock and black pyjamas. She looked bewildered. Her eyes met Karl's. Karl turned away. But he could still see her eyes. He whirled, dropped to one knee, took careful aim, and shot her head off. He thought: They've all got to die now. What have they got to live for, anyway? He was putting them out of their misery. He thought: If I don't shoot them, they'll see that it was me who shot the others. He reached up and pulled his helmet more firmly over his eyes. It was not his fault. They had told him he would be shooting VC. It was too late, now.

They left the hamlet and were on a road. They saw a whole lot of women and children in a ditch between the road and a paddy field. Karl was the first to fire at them. Leinster finished them off with his grenades. Only Karl and Leinster had bothered to fire that time. Nobody looked at anybody else for a moment. Then Grossman said: "It's a VC village. All we're doing is stopping them from growing up to be VC."

Leinster snorted. "Yeah."

163

"It's true," said Sergeant Grossman. He looked around him at the paddy-fields as if addressing the hundreds of hidden VC he thought must be there. "Its true. We've got to waste them all this time."

Another group of men emerged on the other side of the paddy-field. They had two grenade launchers which they were firing at random into the ground and making the mud and plants gout up.

Karl looked at the corpses in the ditch. They were really mangled.

They went back into the village. They found a hut with three old women in it. They wasted the hut and its occupants. They found a two-year-old kid, screaming. They wasted him. They found a fifteen-year-old girl. After Leinster and another man called Aitken had torn her clothes off and raped her, they wasted her. Karl didn't fuck her because he couldn't get a hard-on, but he was the one who shot her tits to ribbons.

"Jesus Christ!" grinned Karl as he and Leinster paused for a moment. "What a day!"

They both laughed. They wasted two water-buffalo and a cow. Leinster blew a hole in the cow with his launcher. "That's a messy cow!" said Karl.

Karl and Leinster went hunting. They were looking for anything which moved. Karl was haunted by the faces of the living. These, and not the dead, were the ghosts that had to be exorcised. He would not be accused by them. He kicked aside the corpses of women to get at their babies. He bayonetted the babies. He and Leinster went into the jungle and found some wounded kids. They wasted the kids as they tried to stumble away.

They went back to the village and found Lieutenant Snider talking to Captain Heffer. They were laughing, too. Captain Heffer's pants were covered in mud to the thigh. He had evidently been in one of the paddies.

The gunships and communications choppers were still thundering away overhead. Every two or three minutes you heard gunfire from somewhere. Karl couldn't see any more gooks. For a moment he had an impulse to shoot Lieutenant Snider and Captain Heffer. If they had turned and seen him, he might have done so. But Leinster tapped him on the shoulder, as if he guessed what he was thinking, and jerked his thumb to indicate they should try the outlying hootches. Karl went with him part of the way, but he had begun to feel tired. He was hoping the battle would be over soon. He saw an unshattered coke bottle lying on the ground. He reached out to pick it up before it occurred to him that it might be booby-trapped. He looked at it for a long time, struggling with his desire for a drink and his caution.

He trudged along the alley between the ruined huts, the sprawled and shattered corpses. Why hadn't the VC appeared? It was their fault. He had been geared to fight. he sound of gunfire went on and on and on.

Karl found that he had left the village. He thought he had better try to rejoin his squad. They ought to retain military discipline. It was the only way to make sense of this. He tried to go back, but he couldn't. He dropped his rifle. He leant down to pick it up. On either side of him the rice paddies gleamed in the sun. He reached out for the rifle, but his boot caught it by accident and it fell into a ditch. He climbed into the ditch to get the rifle. He found it. I was covered in slime. He knew it would take him an age to clean it. He realised that he had begun to cry. He sat in the ditch and he shook with weeping.

A little later Grossman found him.

Grossman kneeled at the side of the ditch and patted Karl's shoulder. "What's the matter, boy?"

Karl couldn't answer.

"Come on, son," said Grossman kindly. He picked Karl's slimy rifle out of the ditch and slung it over his own shoulder. "There ain't much left to do here." He helped Karl to his feet. Karl drew a deep, shuddering breath.

"Don't worry, kid," said Grossman. "Please ..."

He seemed to be begging Karl, as if Karl were reminding him of something he didn't want to remember.

"Now, you stop all that, you hear? It ain't manly." He

spoke gruffly and kept patting Karl's shoulder, but there was an edge to his voice, too.

"Sorry," said Karl at last as they moved back to the village.

"Nobody's blaming you," said the sergeant. "Nobody's blaming nobody. It's what happens, that's all."

"I'm sorry," said Karl again.

– *But we have got to blame somebody sooner or later, says Karl. – We need victims. Somebody's got to suffer. "Now, lieutenant, will you kindly tell the Court just what you had to do with the Human Condition? We are waiting, lieutenant? Why are we not as happy as we might be, lieutenant? Give your answer briefly and clearly."*

– *What the hell are you talking about? says his friend, waking up and yawning.*

– *I didn't say anything, says Karl. – You must have been dreaming. Do you feel better?*

– *I'm not sure.*

– *You don't look it.*

What Would You Do? (17)

You have been travelling in the desert.

There has been an accident. Your car has overturned and the friend with whom you were travelling has been badly hurt. He is almost certain to die.

Would you remain with him and hope that rescue would come soon?

Would you leave him what water you have, making him as comfortable as possible and setting off to find help, knowing he will probably he dead by the time you return?

Would you decide that, since he was as good as dead. you might as well take the water and food with you, as it will give you a better chance?

Would you remain in the shade of the wreck, knowing that this would be the wisest thing to do, but deciding not to waste your water on your dying friend?

18

London Life: 1990: City of Shadows

One of the happiest answers recorded of living states-
men was that in which a well known minister recommended to an alarmed interrogator "the study
of large maps". The danger which seems so im-
minent, so ominous, when we read about it in a newspaper article or in the report of a speech, grows
reassuringly distant when considered through the
medium of a good sized chart.

HER MAJESTY'S ARMY: INDIAN AND COLONIAL FORCES.
A Descriptive Account, by Walter Richards,
J. S. Virtue & Co., 1890.

If SNCC had said Negro Power or Colored Power,
white folks would've continued sleeping easy every
night. But BLACK POWER! Black! That word.
BLACK! And the visions came of alligator-infested
swamps arched by primordial trees with moss drip-
ping from the limbs and out of the depths of the
swamp, the mire oozing from his skin, came the black
monster and fathers told their daughters to be in by
nine instead of nine-thirty. The visions came of big
BLACK bucks running through the streets, raping
everything white that wore a dress, burning, stealing,
killing. BLACK POWER! My God, the niggers were
gon' start paying white folks back. They hadn't forgotten 14-year-old Emmett Till being thrown into

the Tallahatchie River. (We know what you and that chick threw off the Tallahatchie bridge, Billy Joe) with a gin mill tied around his ninety-pound body. They hadn't forgotten the trees bent low with the weight of black bodies on a lyching rope. They hadn't forgotten the black women walking down country roads who were shoved into cars, raped, and then pushed out, the threat of death ringing in their ears, the pain of hateful sex in their pelvis. The niggers hadn't forgotten and they wanted power. BLACK POWER!

LOOK OUT, WHITEY! BLACK POWER'S GON' GET YOUR MAMA *by Julius Lester, Allison & Busby, 1970*

— It's dawn, says Karl. — At last! I'm starving!

— You're beautiful, says his friend.   I want you for always.

— Well . . .

— Always.

— Let's have some breakfast. What's the time? Do they serve it yet?

— They serve it whenever you want it, whatever you want.

— That's service.

— Karl?

— What?

— Please stay with me.

— I think I'll just have something simple. Boiled eggs and toast. Christ, can you hear my stomach rumbling?

Karl is fifty-one. Lonely. All as far as he can see the ruins stretch away, some black, some grey, some red, outlined against a cold sky. The world is over.

Karl's friend seizes him by the wrist. The grip hurts Karl, he tries to break free. Karl blinks. The pain swims through him, confusing him.

An old fifty-one. A scrawny fifty-one. And what has he survived for? What right has he had to survive when others have not? There is no justice . . .

168

– Karl, you promised me, last night.

*– I don't remember much of last night. It was a bit con-
fused, last night, wasn't it?*

– Karl! I'm warning you.

*Karl smiles, taking an interest in his fine, black body.
He turns one of his arms this way and that as the dawn sunshine glints on the rich, shiny skin. – That's nice, he says.*

*– After all I've done for you, says his friend, almost
weeping.*

*– There's no justice, says Karl. – Or maybe there is a
very little. Maybe you have to work hard to manufacture
tiny quantities of justice, the way you get gold by panning
for it. Eh?*

*– There's only desire! His friend hisses through savage,
stained teeth. His eyes are bloodshot. – Karl! Karl! Karl!*

*– You're looking even worse in the daylight, says Karl.
– You could do with some breakfast as much as me. Let's
order it now. We can talk while we eat.*

KARL WILL BE FIFTY-ONE. His mother will have been dead
long-since, of cancer. His father will have been dead for
eight years, killed in the Wolverhampton riots of 1982. Karl
will be unemployed.

He will sit by the shattered window of his front room on
the ground floor of the house in Ladbroke Grove, London.
He will look out into the festering street. There will be nobody there but the rats and the cats. There will be only a
handful of other human beings left in London, most of them
in Southwark, by the River.

But the wars will be over. It will be peaceful.

Peaceful for Karl, at any rate. Karl will have been a can-
nibal for two of the years he has been home, having helped
in the Destruction of Hong Kong and served as a mercenary
in Paris, where he will have gained the taste for human
flesh. Anything will be preferable to the rats and the cats.
Not that, by this time, he will be hunting his meat himself;
he will have lost any wish to kill the few creatures like him
who will haunt the diseased ruins of the city.

Karl will brood by the window. He will have secured all other doors and windows against attack, though there will have been no attack up to that time. He will have left the wide window open, since it will command the best view of Ladbroke Grove.

He will have been burning books in the big fireplace to keep himself warm. He will not, any longer, be reading books. They will all depress him too much. He will not, as far as it will be possible, think any more. He will wish to become only a part of whatever it will be that he is part of.

From the corners of his eyes he will see fleeting shadows which he will think are people, perhaps even old friends who will have come, seeking him out. But they will only be shadows. Or perhaps rats. Or cats. But probably only shadows. He will come to think of these shadows in quite an affectionate way. He will see them as the ghosts of his unborn children. He will see them as the women he never loved, the men he never knew.

Karl will scratch his scurvy, unhealthy body. His body will be dying much faster now that the cans will have run out and he will no longer be able to find the tablets of vitamins he has used before.

He will not fear death.

He will not understand death, just as he will not understand life.

One idea will run together with another.

Nothing will have a greater or a lesser value than another thing. All will have been brought to the same state. This will be peace of a particular kind. This will be security and stability of a particular kind. There will be no other kind who will have come, seeking him out. But they will only be neither content nor discontented as the time will pass. All things will flow together. There will be no past, no present, no future.

Later Karl will lie like a lizard, unmoving on the flat table, his rifle forgotten beside him, and he will stare out at the ruins as if he has known them all his life, as if they, like him, are eternal.

They eat breakfast.

– It's a lovely morning, says Karl.

– I am very rich, says his friend. – I can let you have all you want. Women, other men, anyone. Power. You can satisfy every desire. And I will be whatever you want me to be. I promise. I will serve you. I will be like a geni from the lamp bringing you your heart's every whim! It is true, Karl! The sickly eyes burn with a fever of lust.

– I'm not sure I want anything at the moment. Karl finishes his coffee.

– Stay with me, Karl.

Karl feels sorry for his friend. He puts down his napkin.

– I'll tell you what we'll do today. We'll go back to the roof garden. What about it?

– If that's what you want.

– I'm very grateful to you, in a way, says Karl.

What Would You Do? (18)

Your father has been to hospital at his doctor's request, because he has been suffering pain in his chest, his stomach and his throat. The hospital has told him that he has a form of rheumatism and prescribes certain kinds of treatment.

You receive a request from your father's doctor to visit him.

The doctor tells you that your father is actually suffering from inoperable cancer. He has cancer of the lung, of the stomach and of the throat. He has at very most a year to live.

The doctor says that the decision whether to tell your father of this is up to you. He, the doctor, can't accept the responsibility.

Your father loves life and he fears death.

Would you tell your father the whole truth?

Would you offer him part of the truth and tell him that he has a chance of recovering?

Would you think it better for your father's peace of mind that he know nothing?

19

In The Roof Garden: 1971: Happy Day

The prosecution today won its fight to try Capt.
Ernest L. Medina on murder charges, but decided not
to seek the death penalty.

INTERNATIONAL HERALD TRIBUNE, *June 26-27, 1971.*

KARL and his friends stood together by the railing, looking
at the view over London. It was a beautiful, warm day.
Karl breathed in the scents of the flowers, of the store below, of the traffic beyond. He felt contented.

His friend's pale, blue eyes were troubled. He looked
thin and his silk suit hardly seemed to fit any longer. He
had put on several rings and, when he tapped his fingers
nervously on the rails, they seemed to be the only part of
him that had any life.

"Are you sure you know what you're doing, Karl?" said
his friend.

"I think so. Honestly, it would be for the best now. It
couldn't last."

"I could do so much for you still. If you knew who I
really was, you'd believe me."

"Oh, I've seen your pictures. I didn't want to put you

out by mentioning it. I didn't recognise you at first, that was all."

"I offered you an empire, and you've chosen a cabbage patch."

Karl grinned. "It's more my style, boss."

"You can always change your mind."

"I know. Thank you."

Karl's friend was reluctant to say goodbye, but he was too miserable to attempt to summon any further strength and try to persuade Karl.

Karl adjusted the hat he had bought for himself on the way up. "I think I'll go down and buy a suit somewhere now," he said. "Adios!"

The white man nodded and turned away without saying goodbye.

"Look after yourself," said Karl. "Get some sleep." With a spring in his step, he walked through the Woodland Garden to the exit. The two middle-aged ladies were there as usual. A fat tourist came out of the lift and bumped into him. The tourist cursed him and then apologised almost at the same time. He was evidently embarrassed.

"Don't worry, boss," said Karl, flashing him a grin. "That's okay."

He took the lift down, changed as usual at the third floor, went down to the ground floor, bought himself a newspaper and studied the lists of runners for the day's races.

A middle-aged man in a check suit and wearing a smart bowler, with a white handle-bar moustache, smelling of tobacco, asked: "What are you planning to do?" He was genuinely interested. He had his own paper open at the racing page. "Any tips?"

"I'm feeling lucky today." Karl ran his slender brown finger down the lists. "What about Russian Roulette, two-thirty, Epsom."

"Right. And thank you very kindly."

"It's all right, man."

The punter laughed heartily and slapped Karl on the back. "I'll say that for you fellows, you know how to keep cheerful. Cheerio!"

Karl saluted and left the store, crossing the High Street and walking up Church Street, enjoying the morning. At Notting Hill he stopped and wondered if he should go straight back to Ladbroke Grove. The suit he wanted had just taken shape in his mind.

See opposite

Recommended Further Reading

BEHOLD THE MAN
Allison & Busby, 1969

THE FINAL PROGRAMME
Allison & Busby, 1969

A CURE FOR CANCER
Allison & Busby, 1971

THE WARLORD OF THE AIR
New English Library, 1971

THE ENGLISH ASSASSIN
Allison & Busby, 1972

THE NATURE OF CATASTROPHE
Hutchinson, 1971

and see also references quoted in above books

T035 794	HOW GREEN WAS MY VALLEY	*Richard Llewellyn*	95p
T039 560	I BOUGHT A MOUNTAIN	*Thomas Firbank*	90p
T033 988	IN THE TEETH OF THE EVIDENCE	*Dorothy L. Sayers*	90p
T040 755	THE KING MUST DIE	*Mary Renault*	85p
T038 149	THE CARPETBAGGERS	*Harold Robbins*	£1.50
T040 917	TO SIR WITH LOVE	*E. R. Braithwaite*	75p
T041 719	HOW TO LIVE WITH A NEUROTIC DOG	*Stephen Baker*	75p
T040 925	THE PRIZE	*Irving Wallace*	£1.65
T034 755	THE CITADEL	*A. J. Cronin*	£1.10
T034 674	STRANGER IN A STRANGE LAND	*Robert Heinlein*	£1.20
T037 673	BABY & CHILD CARE	*Dr Benjamin Spock*	£1.50
T037 053	79 PARK AVENUE	*Harold Robbins*	£1.25
T035 697	DUNE	*Frank Herbert*	£1.25
T035 832	THE MOON IS A HARSH MISTRESS	*Robert Heinlein*	£1.00
T040 933	THE SEVEN MINUTES	*Irving Wallace*	£1.50
T038 130	THE INHERITORS	*Harold Robbins*	£1.25
T035 689	RICH MAN, POOR MAN	*Irwin Shaw*	£1.50
T037 134	EDGE 27: DEATH DRIVE	*George Gilman*	75p
T037 541	DEVIL'S GUARD	*Robert Elford*	£1.25
T038 386	THE RATS	*James Herbert*	75p
T030 342	CARRIE	*Stephen King*	75p
T033 759	THE FOG	*James Herbert*	80p
T033 740	THE MIXED BLESSING	*Helen van Slyke*	£1.25
T037 061	BLOOD AND MONEY	*Thomas Thompson*	£1.50